PUPPY PATROL ™

BEST OF FRIENDS

JENNY DALE

Illustrations by Mick Reid
Cover illustration by Michael Rowe

AN
APPLE
PAPERBACK

SCHOLASTIC INC.
New York   Toronto   London   Auckland   Sydney
Mexico City   New Delhi   Hong Kong   Buenos Aires

SPECIAL THANKS TO MARGARET MCALLISTER

If you purchased this book without a cover, you should be aware that this book is stolen property. It was reported as "unsold and destroyed" to the publisher, and neither the author nor the publisher has received any payment for this "stripped book."

No part of this publication may be reproduced in whole or in part, or stored in a retrieval system, or transmitted in any form, or by any means, electronic, mechanical, photocopying, recording, or otherwise, without written permission of the publisher. For information regarding permission, write to Macmillan Publishers Ltd., 25 Eccleston Place, London SW1W 9NF and Basingstoke.

ISBN 0-439-31910-2

Text copyright © 1998 by Working Partners Limited.
Illustrations copyright © 1998 by Mick Reid.

All rights reserved. Published by Scholastic Inc., 555 Broadway,
New York, NY 10012 by arrangement with Macmillan Children's Books,
a division of Macmillan Publishers Ltd.

SCHOLASTIC and associated logos are trademarks and/or registered trademarks of Scholastic Inc.

24 23 22 21 20 19 18 17 16 15 14   10 11 12 13 14 15 /0

Printed in the U.S.A.   40
First Scholastic printing, February 2002

CHAPTER ONE

Neil Parker scribbled furiously in his notebook as he listened attentively to the young SPCA inspector. He was fascinated.

"The last time I was in any real danger," said Terri McCall, leaning back on her chair behind her desk, "was when I had to take an exotic-looking Afghan hound to a quarantine kennel. The owner threatened to slash the tires of my van and have his dog attack me."

Neil gasped and looked up.

"I thought I could handle the dog," Terri continued, "but I wasn't sure about the owner." Terri waited for him to catch up. She saw him hesitate and quickly scribbled on a piece of paper. "That's the correct spelling of quarantine," she said. "Now, what else do you want to know? Any more questions? Chris, what about you?"

Chris Wilson, Neil's best friend from Meadowbank School, was sitting beside him and nodded his head. "How —?"

But a telephone rang in the next room and Terri motioned with her hand that he should hold on a moment.

"I'll be right back," said Terri, leaving Neil and Chris to look around the Padsham SPCA office, with its charts and animal posters plastered all over the walls.

"Funny way for us to spend a Saturday morning," said Chris, looking around at the posters. There was a faint smell of disinfectant in the air. "She's cool, though, isn't she?"

Neil and Chris didn't often use the word "cool" when they did their homework, but this was different. Everyone in Meadowbank School had to write an article for the spring edition of the school magazine, but only the best were going to be published. Neil and Chris were spending some of their free time interviewing Terri about her work with animals.

"There's no way I could do her job," said Chris. "She must be tougher than she looks. She's been pecked by parrots, bitten by frightened dogs, clawed by cats . . .What are you writing?"

Neil was scrawling *Dog in Dramatic Rescue* in large capital letters in his notebook. He frowned and scratched his head with the end of his pen, so that his spiky brown hair stuck out in all directions.

"I want to get a top grade," he said. "I'm going to write the best article ever. A total scoop!"

"Get real," said Chris. "It'll never happen. And," he added, looking at Neil's notes, "that's not how you spell Afghan."

"Oh. Well, here's Terri again. I'll ask her how it's spelled."

But Terri was already reaching for her shoulder bag. "Dog emergency, I'm afraid," she said, grabbing her coat and car keys. "It's in Compton. I have to go immediately, but you two can come with me if you promise to do exactly as you're told."

Neil and Chris exchanged excited glances and scrambled to get their things together.

Dogs meant the world to Neil. His parents ran King Street Kennels, a boarding kennel with a rescue center, just outside Compton. Neil couldn't imagine a better way of life.

With Chris behind him, Neil climbed into the SPCA van. Then Terri set off on the road to Compton.

"This isn't really my sort of case," she said, as she drove. "But I promised to help an old friend. Her name's Maude Lumley."

Neil frowned. He knew that name from somewhere but he couldn't remember where.

"Maude is always taking in stray dogs," Terri explained. "She's consulted me about them in the past. She can't shut her door on any dog that needs a little love. But I haven't heard from her in ages."

"So has she taken in another stray?" Neil imagined a neglected dog in need of food and kindness.

"Well — no, she hasn't," said Terri. "I told you it wasn't really my kind of case. It isn't about a dog at all."

Neil's face fell. This wasn't going to be a dramatic dog rescue after all.

"Maude's fallen down the stairs and hurt her arm."

"Is she OK?" asked Chris. "Why didn't she send for the doctor?"

"She's very wary of doctors," said Terri. "Almost afraid of them. I suppose you could say Maude is a bit eccentric. But she knows me and trusts me, so she's asked me to help. And, if she has to go to the hospital, she knows I can arrange to have her dogs looked after while she's away."

Neil's face lit up again. "We'll take them!" he said enthusiastically. Neil would do anything to help a dog — like the frightened, hungry strays brought in to the rescue center. His own Border collie, Sam, had been a stray when he first arrived at King Street. Sam had recently developed a heart condition, and this made him even more important in Neil's life. Neil would adopt every stray dog he met if he could. "We've got room for more at King Street Kennels, if you need it."

"We haven't even gotten there yet," laughed Terri. "It's strange — I used to see Maude out walking all the time, but not anymore. You can spot her a mile away — she's got a shock of white hair and always has a collection of different dogs around her, all yapping and barking. I'm sure you'd recognize her."

"Oh, her!" said Neil as he remembered who Maude Lumley was. "The dog woman. I've seen her at Mike Turner's veterinary clinic."

"Let's see," murmured Terri, as they approached a junction. "Windsor Drive is on the left, isn't it?"

"That's right," said Neil. "We might even see Emily. She's interviewing the Jepsons for *her* magazine article. They have two very spoiled Westies named Sugar and Spice. They are the naughtiest dogs I know!"

Neil's sister Emily was as obsessed with dogs as he was.

"Windsor Drive," said Chris. "Isn't that where all the gardens are really fancy? My mom says it's like walking through the Chelsea Flower Show."

"And she's right! Look!" said Terri, as they turned onto a street of expensive-looking terraced houses. Most had elegant porches and smart white conservatories. Even now, in winter, many gardens had green lawns and clusters of shrubs trimmed into neat shapes. "Look for number twenty-four."

Neil leaned forward, counting house numbers. "It's that one!" he said.

"What a mess!" exclaimed Chris.

Number 24 stood out from the rest of the homes on Windsor Drive, as if it didn't belong there. The paint was dirty and peeling away. What was left of the lawn was thin and patchy, and in the flowerbeds were a few neglected bushes. Two or three battered, old rubber bones and the remains of a football littered the path.

The brakes of Terri's van squeaked a little as she parked outside the gate. This set off the sound of excited barking inside the house. Some were gruff and some were high-pitched. Neil thought he could hear at least five different dogs.

"Oh no. She hasn't cleaned up after them very

well," said Terri, frowning as she jumped down from the van and looked around the garden. "That's odd. It looks as if her dogs have had the run of this place for months. You two stay in the van. Mrs. Lumley isn't expecting anyone else. Besides," she muttered, "who knows what it's like in there, if the garden's anything to judge by."

There was more barking as Terri banged the van door shut and walked up the path.

"All this noise has annoyed the neighbors," said Chris, pointing through the front window. "Look at those two."

Neil turned to see a large man in a tweed jacket with a small woman beside him, watching from the other side of the street. Neil guessed that the balding man was between sixty and seventy. His wife, a tiny figure by comparison, had a worried expression on her face and stood fussing and fidgeting with her gloves. The man frowned and pointed at the van, whispered to his wife, took a notebook from his pocket, and scribbled something down.

Neil jumped from the van. "Where's Terri gone? She must have gone in around the back."

"And she's let something out!" said Chris. "Look!"

Bounding at full-speed toward Neil from the side of the house came a spaniel, barking with furious excitement. It raced toward the low garden wall, its floppy ears dancing up and down energetically.

Neil instinctively ran to meet the dog.

"Watch out!" yelled Chris — but it was too late. With wildly flailing legs, the dog leaped into the air, easily cleared the wall, and landed eagerly in front of Neil. As he bent down to say hello, the dog enthusiastically started licking his face.

"Whoa! Where did you come from?" laughed Neil. He turned his face to avoid the dog's slobbery tongue.

Chris began searching for a leash as Neil caught hold of her collar and tried to keep her under control.

"Good dog. Calm down," said Neil. "You're an excitable thing, aren't you, girl?" He patted the dog's

head and quickly looked her over as she struggled to break free. He noticed that her coat was dirty and matted.

Chris came forward and attached a leash to the dog's collar. "She smells a bit, doesn't she?" He held his nose and laughed.

"You're right," said Neil, smiling. Then he looked more serious. "She looks as if she might have ringworm. I'm not certain." Neil fished a pair of old gloves from his pocket and put them on. "Try not to touch her too much."

Chris wiped his hands on his jeans. "Now you tell me!"

Neil ruffled the dog's matted fur and began to examine her more closely. The smile on his face faded and he began to look angry. "I thought Maude Lumley was supposed to be a dog lover. This dog's got sores on her skin, and her ears are filthy. She could easily get an infection." The dog's coat was straggly, with round patches of bare skin around her paws and ears. "Good girl, you're all right now," he soothed.

"She'll be a nice-looking dog when she's cleaned up," said Chris.

Neil grinned as the black-and-white dog jumped up at him again. He handed the leash to Chris. "Will you get her into the back of the van and stay with her? I'm going to find out what's going on."

As he walked down the path toward the house, a

breeze wafted across the neglected garden and a pungent smell assaulted Neil's nose. He couldn't help making a face. There were up to fifty dogs at a time at King Street Kennels, and it never smelled anything like that. But King Street had the Parker family and Kate, their kennel assistant, to keep it clean. Number 24 Windsor Drive looked as if it didn't have anybody.

The stale, sour smell of the house got stronger as Neil peered through a practically open grimy window into the living room. His attention immediately went to a golden Labrador standing on its hind legs, pawing at the closed door inside. Next to the Labrador, a scruffy Yorkshire terrier scrabbled and yapped furiously. The Labrador began to whine in distress, and Neil wondered where Terri could be. An enormous hairy mongrel was sprawled across a saggy old sofa, a half-chewed slipper beside it.

That's three, thought Neil. *And the one in the van makes four.*

All the furniture seemed to have suffered from so many dogs. Neil noticed scratched wood and paintwork. The chair covers looked ragged and rumpled, as if the dogs had pawed them through. The edges of the carpet had been scratched up. From behind a chair, a small, dark-colored terrier limped toward the window, fiercely barking at Neil. It made a brave attempt to put its paws up on the windowsill, but its lame leg failed and it dropped down again. Neil wanted desperately to help it.

"It won't be long now," he said, hoping the dog would hear him and feel reassured. "We'll get you out soon." Anger bubbled up inside him. How many more could there be?

Neil's attention had been wholly absorbed by the dogs, but the uneasy feeling that he was being watched made him turn around. A group of neighbors had gathered on the sidewalk. In spite of the sharp, cold air, they stood around whispering and waiting to see what would happen next.

As Neil walked back to the van, there was a friendly wave from a small, dark-haired figure in the crowd, and his sister Emily ran to meet him. The spaniel in the van kept up a loud and steady barking.

"Mrs. Jepson was showing me her hanging baskets when I saw the van," said Emily, looking relieved to have an excuse to get away. "What's going on?"

Neil tried to explain, but they were interrupted when a large, tweedy man marched up to join them.

"I'm Mr. Crosby," he said. He had a gruff, rather bossy way of speaking and struggled to raise his voice above the protesting spaniel. Neil could see that Mr. Crosby didn't like to be argued with.

"It's good to see something's being done at last," the man said in a loud voice. "I've complained to the

Environmental Health Officer about this house, I
don't know how many times! It's shocking. All that
barking! That one in the van, does it ever stop? It up-
sets my wife, you know. She doesn't like to get too
close to any of them, do you, Muriel? Is the SPCA
taking the dogs away?"

Neil was saved from having to answer him by
the appearance of an ambulance, which set off more
whispers and speculation among the small crowd.
Neil ran to meet the young paramedic who approached the gate.

"It's Mrs. Lumley," Neil explained as he shep-
herded the man toward the side of the house. "She's
hurt her arm. Did Terri McCall send for you? I'll
show you where to find them."

Neil's attempt to get into the house failed. The
paramedic shut the back door firmly behind him, but
not before Neil caught sight of a kitchen with dirty
curtains, empty cans of dog food, and unwashed
dishes piled up in the sink. He could hear whining
coming from inside somewhere and paws scrabbling
at a door. Digging his hands into his pockets, he
marched back to the van as a second paramedic carried a wheelchair to the door. He pulled Emily to one
side.

"Dad will have a fit when he finds out about this,"
he said, and glared at the house. "Mrs. Lumley asked
for help for herself, but not for those dogs! One of

them is limping. She shouldn't ever be allowed near —"

A terrible sound stopped him: the howling and yelping of a dog in pain.

Neil turned and ran back to the house.

CHAPTER TWO

The front door opened just as Neil reached it.

"What . . . ?" He gasped. The howling dog was the little Yorkshire terrier Neil had seen through the front window. It was pulling and straining with all its might as Terri struggled to control it on one leash and a Labrador on another.

"Take the Lab, would you please, Neil," Terri shouted above the noise. "The Yorkie is OK, don't worry. Apparently he always makes this racket when he first gets his leash on. He'll calm down when he gets moving — or so I'm told."

The Yorkie certainly didn't appear to be in pain, just wildly overexcited. His coat was patchy and matted — just like the spaniel's — but his eyes were bright and his ears sharply pricked up.

Chris plugged his ears with his fingers. "What a noise!"

The Labrador was much more relaxed but padded along stiffly at Neil's side as he walked her to the van. Neil was puzzled about her. She looked young — her coat was a rich gold with no sign of whitening around the muzzle — but she walked slowly and awkwardly, as if she were old and tired.

Terri followed him with the yapping Yorkie, whose outbursts began to become more intermittent. The spaniel, shut in the front of Terri's van, heard him and was barking frantically in reply. There was a great scuffling and bumping in the van, as if she were determined to get out, and she scratched furiously on the window. Her claws rattled on the glass.

"I'll see if she's all right," said Emily.

"Be careful," said Neil, as Terri unlocked the back of the van. "The spaniel might have ringworm, so don't touch her."

Emily didn't want to risk catching ringworm again. She'd had it before and it was unbearable. It had been horrible not being able to scratch an itch for two weeks!

Then the paramedics emerged from the house.

"Looks like they've persuaded Mrs. Lumley to come out," said Terri.

Neil turned a scowling face toward the house. It was difficult for him to feel sympathy for Maude Lumley.

Two paramedics eased a wheelchair gently over the doorstep, taking care not to let it bump. It was hard to see the face of the small woman slumped in the chair. Her head hung down, and she was shaking as if in shock. Her injured arm was in a temporary sling, and a blanket had been tucked over her knees. At the gate, she turned her head and said something to Terri, who squatted down beside her to listen. The Yorkie wagged his tail and nuzzled her leg.

"Poor old thing," said Chris. "She looks terrible."

Mrs. Lumley's voice was weak. Neil moved in

closer to hear what was going on and the Labrador sat faithfully beside her.

"I'm not going anywhere," Mrs. Lumley was saying. Her voice was shaky but determined. "I can't leave until I know my dogs are being properly looked after."

Properly looked after? thought Neil. *After the way she's treated them!*

"I've told you, Maude," said Terri. "I'll take good care of your dogs."

"But if you take them, I won't get them back!" Mrs. Lumley's eyes filled with tears.

"That's not necessarily so," said Terri, but Mrs. Lumley wouldn't listen.

"Couldn't you just arrange something? Someone to just help out a bit?" pleaded Mrs. Lumley. "If the SPCA takes my dogs, I'll never see them again!" With one hand she gripped an arm of the wheelchair as she struggled to stand, swayed, and was gently settled down again by a paramedic. "It's no good, I just can't think of it. They'd miss me so much. Poor little Yap, and Ludo, and Spangle . . ."

"King Street Kennels could take them," said Neil, flatly.

Terri and Mrs. Lumley looked at him.

Terri nodded. "If you really don't want to sign them over to me, it might be the best thing to do," she agreed. She tucked the blanket more snugly over

Mrs. Lumley's knees. "Do you know King Street Kennels, Maude? Bob and Carole Parker?"

"Oh!" A hopeful light came into Mrs. Lumley's eyes, and she reached out and placed a hand on Neil's arm. "Are you Bob's boy, then?"

"Yes, he's my dad," said Neil.

"Is he?" said Mrs. Lumley, with a shaky smile. "That nice tall man? I used to take my dogs to his training classes, years ago, when I could . . . when I went to things like that." Neil wondered why she'd stopped. "Yes," Maude continued. "He's very good with dogs. I'd like him to look after my family." Puzzled, she looked around, then looked at Neil.

"Where's Spangle? Did she run away?"

"Spangle?"

"Spangle the spaniel. I can hear her somewhere."

"She's in the van. She's safe."

"Will you let me have a key to your house, Maude?" asked Terri. "Then I can lock up after I've loaded up all the dogs." They all waited, shuffling their feet and rubbing their hands in the cold, while Mrs. Lumley hunted in a battered old handbag for a bunch of keys.

"I'll need to take someone in with me, as a witness," said Terri, as Mrs. Lumley finally found her keys. "It's an SPCA rule that inspectors don't go into a house alone when the owner isn't there. Perhaps Bob Parker could come and help with the dogs at the same time."

"Let's go. We need to get you into the ambulance," insisted one of the paramedics. "It's too cold to have you sitting around out here."

"Yes, yes, in a minute," fussed Mrs. Lumley, turning back to Terri. "The Labrador is Ludo. She's a bit stiff but I don't know why. And the little Yorkie is Yap. I'm afraid he's noisy, but he can't help it. He gets excited, especially when he's going for a walk. Quiet, Yap!" Yap ignored her and went on living up to his name. "And the very big dog, he's Sean, and there's Pippin. Pippin has a lame leg. Oh dear," she closed her eyes and drooped weakly in the chair, her voice fading to a whisper. "I feel dizzy."

"Hospital. Now," said the paramedic, and firmly pushed the wheelchair into the ambulance.

"Don't worry," called Terri. "We'll take good care of your dogs, won't we, Neil?"

As the ambulance drove away, Yap, with fast and furious yelps, strained at the leash to follow it, then changed his mind and scratched frantically at a sore spot. Ludo sighed and lay down on the pavement, her head on her paws. The inquisitive neighbors slowly drifted away — all except for Mr. Crosby, who stopped to talk to Terri.

"It's about time, too," he said. "I'm glad you were called in at last. I take it we'll see no more of these dogs now."

"I really can't say anything definite about that, sir," said Terri. Yap finally stopped barking and started a miserable whining. "The dogs still belong to Mrs. Lumley."

Mr. Crosby's face reddened. "Aren't you going to bring charges against her?"

"I can't discuss that," said Terri firmly.

Neil watched the deepening color of Mr. Crosby's face and wondered if he might turn purple. He clearly hadn't expected Terri to stand up to him. "But you're taking them away, aren't you?" he insisted.

"For the moment, yes. The dogs will be taken from the house today for their own welfare."

"They're coming to King Street Kennels," said Neil.

"I don't care where they go, so long as they're not here," said Mr. Crosby. "It's torture for the rest of us on the block. I'm going to keep an eye on things here. You haven't heard the last of this." And he stamped away.

"Oh dear." Terri sighed. "At least the spaniel's stopped barking, at last."

The Labrador sniffed at Chris's hand. Chris bent down to her.

"Careful," said Terri. "We don't know if she has an infection or not."

"It's hard to resist her, isn't it?" said Chris. "She looks so unhappy. What's her name? Ludo? Funny name for a girl dog. There's a good girl, Ludo. You'll be happy when we get you to King Street. They'll look after you there." Ludo wagged her tail slowly, as if she wasn't at all sure.

"They couldn't go anywhere better," said Terri, as the Yorkie suddenly sat down and began biting at its paw. "Yes, Yap. I know it itches, but leave it alone." Terri moved the dog's mouth away from his paw. "I'll take them to Mike, then they can stay at King Street until we have some definite decisions about their future. I'll be in touch with your father. Are you all going home now?"

"No, I'm supposed to be going back to Chris's for lunch," said Neil.

"And I haven't finished my interview," said Emily.

Terri nodded. "Then I'll take you boys back to my office so you can get your bikes. I'll just take Spangle and these two now, then I'll come back for the others — I can't get them all in one van load. Do you know if there's much room in the rescue center? I know that winter is a bad time of year for abandoned dogs."

"We'll fit them in," said Neil.

"I still don't know exactly how many dogs there are in the house," Terri went on. "Emily, what's the matter?"

Emily had checked that Spangle was all right. Now she came back from the van looking very worried.

"Neil," she said, "maybe you shouldn't have left Spangle in the front of the van."

"The back was locked," Chris said defensively.

"Why?" asked Neil. "What's the matter?"

"Terri," said Emily, "I'm afraid you're not going to like this."

Terri walked over to the front of the van and peered in warily. The upholstery of the roof hung down in tatters, and the seats had been ripped open so that the stuffing spilled out. A large piece of padding was still in her mouth and patches of white fluff stuck to her nose.

"Whoops," said Terri.

Spangle looked at her and sneezed. Then she lay down and dropped the padding apologetically, as if she hoped that would make everything better.

It looked like Spangle had a real behavior problem!

CHAPTER THREE

Saturday lunch at Chris's house wasn't as much fun as usual. Neil couldn't think about anything except Mrs. Lumley's dogs and whether or not they had been rescued yet. He left early and cycled home, taking a long detour via Windsor Drive.

Outside Mrs. Lumley's house, he spotted a green Range Rover with the King Street Kennels logo on the side, parked behind Terri's SPCA van. His dad must already be here.

There was no sign of either Bob Parker or Terri, but Neil could hear a dog barking in the van and another in the house.

On the opposite side of the road Neil saw Mr. Crosby, his collar turned up against the cold and his shoulders hunched. Notebook in hand, he seemed determined not to miss anything.

As Neil jumped off his bike, his father came out of the house. A tall, bearded man, he carried a small dog in his arms — a little terrier that cuddled trustingly against him. With Bob's great height and broad shoulders and the terrier shivering in his arms, he looked like a gentle giant.

"Need any help, Dad?" asked Neil, running over to him.

"Don't handle any of them," said Bob. Neil noticed that his father was wearing protective gloves. "All of these dogs are infested. Fleas, lice, parasites — you name it, they've got it. And this one's got an injury to his paw."

"I saw him this morning," said Neil. "I think his name's Pippin."

"Luckily, I don't think any of them have ringworm. Mike called me and gave the others at the clinic the OK. I suspect Pippin will be OK, too."

The terrier turned his head and twitched his ears at the sound of his name. Bob scratched him gently behind his ears.

"All right, Pippin. Nobody's going to hurt you," he said reassuringly.

Terri emerged from the van and Bob handed the miserable little terrier over to her. "Here's Pippin." A bit skinny with a sore paw, Pippin was not happy.

"That's number six, Terri, and there's still that shaggy rug-like thing. Big, but harmless. I haven't checked upstairs yet."

"Six?" said Neil. "Does that include the ones that Terri took to Mike's clinic this morning?"

Terri smiled. "Yes, it does, and don't remind me. I can still hear that yapping in my head. No wonder the neighbors complained. Mike put Spangle in a very spacious pen but she was already trying to eat her way out by the time I left. She chewed her towel to shreds in no time!"

"And what about Ludo the Lab?" asked Neil.

"I think she has bad arthritis." She made gentle soothing noises to Pippin as she carried him back to her van.

Neil was just about to ask Terri why the Labrador had a boy's name when Mr. Crosby strode across the road and took up the angry questioning he had started earlier that morning.

"Have you decided whether to press charges against that woman? Animal cruelty charges? Look at that dog!"

"I'm sorry, I still can't discuss the case," insisted Terri. "It's cold, and I've got to get these dogs to the kennel as quickly as possible."

Neil opened a pet carrier, but Pippin shrank away from it. With Neil's help, Terri pushed Pippin gently into the carrier and Neil shut it quickly, slipping in a

dog treat from his pocket as he did so. Pippin gob-
bled it up.

"I won't let this rest," said Mr. Crosby. "Your supe-
riors will be hearing from me." He marched home,
stopping to share the latest news with a neighbor.

"That's it — that's all of them," said Bob, when he
led out the enormous shaggy mongrel. The dog hung
its head, and its tail was tucked between its legs. Bob
carried a smooth-haired, chocolate-brown puppy
that shivered in his arms. "I found the pup upstairs
in a bedroom. He probably just learned to climb

stairs and couldn't work out how to get down again, poor thing. He's terrified, and his skin's all sore."

Neil could see the long, painful marks where the puppy had scratched at his flea bites. Neil was used to seeing neglected animals arriving at King Street thin, dirty, and scared, but every single one still made him angry. And he had never seen so many at once, all from the same dismal house. He looked from one pair of helpless brown eyes to another. One made a feeble attempt to wag its tail, the other was biting and scratching at itchy skin. Neil wished there was something he could do.

"Put your bike in the back of the Range Rover," Bob suggested. "We'll get these dogs over to Mike."

Neil roughly heaved the bike in, climbed in next to his dad, and slammed the door so violently that the seat rocked under him.

"Relax, Neil," Bob said quietly.

Neil jerked at the seat belt so hard that it jammed. Finally strapping himself in, he said, "I felt sorry for Mrs. Lumley this morning. That was before I realized the disgusting state of her dogs. I hope she's never allowed near a dog again, ever." He sat with a set, tight face and clenched hands all the way to the vet's office.

Neil felt a lot better later that afternoon when he'd had a shower and changed into some clean clothes. He and his dad had dropped off the last few dogs from Windsor Drive for a checkup at Mike Turner's clinic and had already prepared some pens at the King Street rescue center for their arrival.

As Neil entered the kitchen, Jake, Sam's Border collie pup, bounded up to him with little yips of delight. When Jake's tail wagged, his whole body wagged, too, and it was impossible for him to keep still. Sam watched proudly as Jake rolled over to have his tummy tickled. It was always good to be welcomed home by his dogs, but especially when Neil saw that they were both happy and healthy, after the neglected waifs he had seen earlier that day.

Sitting down to a hot meal made Neil feel better, too. Between mouthfuls of hamburgers and baked beans, he and Emily told their mother, Carole, all that had happened. Their little sister, Sarah, who was five years old, listened carefully.

"Does anyone neglect hamsters?" she asked. She adored her pet hamster, Fudge.

"I'm sure they don't," said Carole firmly, raising an eyebrow at Neil before he could say anything else.

"If they did," went on Sarah, "would they go to prison?"

"I don't know, darling." Carole glanced up at the clock on the wall. "Kate's coming in to help out soon. I told her we had eight new dogs arriving, and that we'd need a massive de-flea session."

As she spoke, there was a knock at the door and a

slim, pony-tailed figure in jeans and a bright, baggy sweater appeared in the doorway.

"Hi, Kate!" said Emily.

"Hi, everyone. I'm going straight over to the rescue center, OK?" said Kate with a smile. "I saw Mike and Terri arriving as I got here. We're going to have fun tonight!"

Neil and Emily gulped down the last of their food and ran out to the rescue center after Kate. Terri and Mike were standing outside in the courtyard by two vans full of noisy dogs. Sarah was soon hurrying along to catch up.

"We've only brought six of them," said Terri. She counted them off on her fingers: "Ludo the Lab, Yap the Yorkie, Spangle the spaniel, Sean the hearthrug, a mongrel called Matt, and one very shaggy terrier. I'm not sure what his name is because he doesn't have a collar. Pippin and the puppy are still at the vet with Janice. Fortunately, Mike had records for some of these dogs."

Mike Turner unlocked the back of his van. "Pippin's paw seems to have an old wound that hasn't healed properly, and the pup can't stop scratching. His skin's a little flaky," he explained. "He probably hasn't had a balanced diet."

"That's horrible!" exclaimed Neil. "Couldn't Mrs. Lumley even bother to look after the puppy?"

"He'll be all right," said Mike. "I'm keeping Pippin and the pup under observation, and they're getting lots of love and attention from Janice. Let's get this bunch settled in. Come and help me with the pet carriers, Neil."

"I didn't think Mrs. Lumley bothered much with vets," said Emily disapprovingly.

"She used to," said Mike, as he opened up the back of the van to a chorus of yaps, barks, and scrabbling noises. "Maude has always taken in strays, and she used to look after them very well. Take the Three Musketeers, for example."

"The what?" said Kate.

"These three — the spaniel, the Lab, and the Yorkie," he said. He stood back as Neil opened the door of a carrier and held out his arms to the dog who scrambled out. "Here's Spangle! Take the leash, Bob, she's very bouncy. And Ludo the Lab. Emily, you can take her."

Spangle shook herself and bounded up to Bob, jumping and dancing for his attention. Ludo, meanwhile, lay down quietly at Emily's feet. Her rich golden coat was patchy with pink skin showing through in places.

"And here's Yap," said Mike. He lifted the little straggle-haired Yorkie from the van, but Yap only wriggled to be put down again. He cowered miserably against a tire.

"Poor thing!" said Kate. She knelt beside him, but he growled and shrank away.

"He's very quiet for a dog called Yap," said Sarah.

"You should have heard him this morning," said Neil.

Sarah looked like she was thinking about something. "He must have used up his yaps," she decided.

"That's right, sweetheart. He's worn out his batteries," said Bob. "So these three have been regular customers of yours, Mike?"

"She's had them a while — kept their injections up to date — even had them wormed regularly. But lately she hadn't brought them in, even when Janice sent reminders."

"Down, Spangle!" said Bob, as Spangle tugged at the leash, darting off in one direction, then another, with her ears flopping and flying. "So, what state are they in?"

"Reasonable, considering. The Yorkie's sulking a bit and the spaniel's full of energy, as you can see."

"What about Ludo?" Neil patted his knees and called the Labrador to him. She stood up with difficulty and lumbered toward him.

"She has osteoarthritis," said Mike. "It's made her hips stiffen up. It's very common in Labs, though she's young to have it so badly. It's usually easy to treat. I'll leave some medication for her. Their skin and fur is in poor condition but I doubt you'll catch anything. A thorough bath with special shampoo is what's needed now."

"So they're not malnourished?" asked Bob.

"No. They've been well fed but just need more of

certain vitamins and definitely more exercise. Let's have them using separate towels for the time being — just in case."

"Which are *not* to be eaten, Spangle," said Terri. Spangle jumped up with excitement at the sound of her name and managed to get her leash caught under her leg.

"Look at you, Spangle," said Neil. He leaned over and gently disentangled her.

Mike went on: "Keep them in isolation for a while and exercise them away from the other dogs. And you must all be very thorough about washing and cleaning your hands when you've been with them. Strict hygiene is important."

Neil was both angry and disappointed that Mrs. Lumley had allowed the dogs to suffer. He shuddered to think how their health might have become worse if their owner hadn't broken her arm.

"Let's get these dogs in the pens," said Bob. "We can't stand here all night. There's another three in Terri's van, including Sean. His mother must have been a wolfhound and his father a woolly mammoth."

"Don't be silly!" said Sarah.

"Wait till you see him," said Kate, who had just looked into the van. "He must stand as tall as Neil's shoulder. Come on, all hands to the treatment block. I hope we've got plenty of shampoo. Rubber gloves and raincoats on!"

Everyone laughed, except Neil.

CHAPTER FOUR

For over an hour, the treatment table and counters of the workroom at King Street Kennels were wet and covered with dogs. None had been groomed for a long time, and there was matted fur to be combed or trimmed away on each one of them.

Bob, Kate, and Terri established a cleaning production line in order to deal with the dogs as efficiently as possible — they each needed a thorough bath, too.

Spangle, who wouldn't stay still, repeatedly escaped from Neil, jumping out of his hands so that water ran down inside his rubber gloves. Once free, she tore around the workroom until everyone was drenched. It took repeated changes of water to wash

Sean, who shook and showered everyone between each rinse.

"Swap, Neil," said Kate, who was patiently massaging shampoo into Yap's paws. "I'll take Spangle, and you have Yap. He might be happier with you." But Yap didn't seem happy with anyone, and the more Neil rinsed his fur, the more sore skin he found. He talked softly to the dog and wished animals could understand English. He hoped a quiet tone of voice would help, but Yap still cowered as Neil wrapped a towel around him and gently rubbed him dry.

By the time they were finished, everyone was soaked through, and their backs ached from bending over the dogs. Spangle had become strangely quiet. It was too late for Neil to save the rubber glove hanging from her mouth and the brush lying beside her, which already had tooth marks in it.

There was still food and water to be given out, and the dogs had to be settled in their pens. It was not a job to be rushed, however tired everyone was feeling. Neil knew that the dogs must find it unsettling to be housed in a strange place, and he stayed as long as he could with Yap. It was then, as he longed to get warm and dry himself, that Neil remembered the heap of wet and dirty towels on the workroom floor. With Bob, he went back to the workroom, where they loaded up the washing machine. Neil banged the door hard and gave the machine a kick as it hummed into life.

"Careful," said Bob.

Neil pretended he hadn't heard. He'd wanted to kick something all day.

Even the short walk back to the house was a cold and weary one. But there was a welcome light in the kitchen, where warmth and hot chocolate waited for them.

"Wherever I go, I'll smell of anti-flea shampoo," muttered Kate, already at the table, cupping her hands around a mug.

"At least the dogs smell a lot better than they did before," said Bob.

"It was like being a doggy hairdresser, Mom — trimming all that matted hair," said Emily.

Bob nodded. "You've both done well there," he said.

"It was a horrible job," mumbled Neil. "Their skin looked so rough, I was afraid of hurting them."

"It's very rewarding," said Kate. "In two weeks you won't recognize them. By the way, Carole, Spangle chewed up a pair of rubber gloves. I hope they didn't do her any harm. My hands weren't in them at the time, I'm happy to say."

"I've got a liquid that will stop Spangle from chewing things," said Bob. "It tastes nasty, but it's harmless. I'll put a few drops on her bedding, to discourage her from eating it."

"You're very quiet, Neil," said Carole. She drew up her chair and sat beside him. "Are you all right?"

"Nothing's all right," Neil said fiercely. "Dogs are very demanding. They need attention, regular exercise, and should have lots of love. If Mrs. Lumley couldn't do that she shouldn't have taken them in the first place. And she pretends she cares about them!"

Terri put down her mug. "It's not as simple as it seems, Neil. I see a lot of cases like Mrs. Lumley. It's because she loves animals so much that she can't turn them away. If a stray dog turns up, she'll look after it. She'll take it in. She'd done that all her life, and, until now, she did it very well. You heard what Mike said."

"That's right, Neil," added Bob. "Maude took on an elderly terrier from the rescue center a few years ago, and she looked after him beautifully."

"She's a widow," continued Kate. "And retired. She's lonely and her dogs are everything to her."

"She used to bring some of them to training classes, too," said Bob. "I thought she must have moved away."

"I think she just can't manage them anymore," said Terri. "She seems to be in bad health herself, so she finds everything hard. And money must be a problem. The house is cold and shabby. She's probably stopped taking dogs to classes and the vet because she can't afford it. I'll bet she feeds the dogs better than she feeds herself."

"Mrs. Lumley could have gotten help," protested Neil. "You would have helped, wouldn't you, Terri? Or Mike. Or we would have. She could have asked, if she really cared about the dogs."

Terri shrugged. "I don't think she liked to ask. She was ashamed of the state she and the dogs were in. She's confused and frightened. Even when she broke her arm she sent for me, not the doctor."

"How did she break her arm?" asked Emily.

"Apparently she tripped on a piece of torn stair carpet. I went to have a look. It was worn very thin, and she said Spangle had been tearing it up. It's a wonder she didn't break her neck, let alone her arm. Of course, she insisted that it wasn't Spangle's fault. She made an effort to feed them this morning, but I'm not sure how well she managed it."

Sam was lying under the table with his head resting against Neil's foot. Neil reached down and scratched behind Sam's ears. Sam's tail beat lazily on the floor. Jake lay fast asleep, his paws twitching a little, trusting and content.

"If I was sick, or anything," Neil said, looking at Sam, "there's always somebody here to look after Sam and Jake."

Neil realized that it was so easy for a dog owner living alone to become injured or ill — and what

happened to their dogs? At least Mrs. Lumley had phoned Terri. "So what will happen now?" he asked.

"I'll visit Mrs. Lumley in the hospital tomorrow," Terri replied. "I'll try to persuade her to sign her dogs over to our care. If she does, I'll take them all to the SPCA rehoming unit."

"Couldn't they stay here until we find homes for them?" said Neil.

"No, Neil, it's SPCA policy that when dogs are signed over we take responsibility for them," said Terri. "And they'll stay there until they go to good homes."

"What if she refuses?"

Terri put her chin in her hands and looked thoughtfully at the table, as if she hoped to find an answer on it.

"I may have to negotiate a little. If she can keep just one or two, she may agree to part with the rest. And I'll keep an eye on things, to make sure she looks after any dogs she does decide to keep. She seems very attached to Ludo and Yap."

"And Spangle," said Emily.

"Yes, and who else would put up with Spangle?" said Bob, then laughed as cries of "I would!" came from all around the table.

"And now I'd better go," said Terri, getting to her feet and reaching for her jacket. "It's late, and it's been a long day. Neil, how is Jake?"

Jake's coat was still puppyish and soft, and he hadn't yet filled out his skin. Curled up asleep, he looked like a cuddly pillow. At the sound of his name he half woke up, gave an enormous yawn, stretched, then padded floppily up to Neil. Neil thought of the new puppy in the rescue center. He had begun to feel just a little sorry for Maude Lumley, but he was still upset when he thought of those dogs.

"Next to Sam he's the best dog in the world," said Neil.

"He certainly is a star, Neil," said Terri. "I'm off. I'll need to throw my uniform in the wash and myself in the bath before I start all over again tomorrow. The things I do for dogs!"

*   *   *

Waking up while it was still dark on Sunday morning, Neil could hear Jake's high-pitched whimper from the kitchen downstairs as the puppy asked to be let out. He was still too young for long walks, but a quick run around the garden was necessary to avoid puddles on the floor. Quickly, Neil put on his clothes and shivered downstairs to the back door. There was frost on the ground, and Jake pounded out into the cold, then galloped back to the shelter of the kitchen.

"That puppy's good for you," said Carole, as she put the kettle on. "He gets you out of bed in the morning."

Neil felt like going back to bed, but by the time he'd eaten, he was fully awake. Emily was downstairs, too, and as it was Bob's day for teaching an obedience class, they offered to start on the morning's dog walking.

"It should be easy for one of us to take Yap and Ludo," said Neil when they got to the rescue block. "But Spangle's a handful."

"I'll take her," said Emily. "If you watch Ludo and the little noisy one."

But the "little noisy one" didn't seem willing to go for a walk at all. Yap cowered back when Neil opened his pen and refused the dog treat held out to him.

"Come on, Yap," coaxed Neil. "It's not that bad."

Yap huddled miserably in his corner. He allowed Neil to stroke him, but there was no wag of the tail or lick of the hand, and he refused to leave the pen. Even the sight of a leash couldn't persuade him to move.

"If you won't, you won't," said Neil sadly, wishing he could do something. "I'll get Ludo while you think about it."

Ludo rose stiffly to meet him. Though she was slow, she walked confidently, wagging her tail and thrusting her muzzle into his hand. Her tail slapped the wire pen in eager anticipation as Neil fastened on the leash. From the wild barking and Emily's laughter in the next pen, he knew that Spangle was ready to go, too. He looked up to see Emily staggering backward and struggling to keep her balance.

"She nearly knocked me over!" cried Emily. "And she's chewed all the bedding. Sit, Spangle!" She gave a gentle shove to put the spaniel's rump into position. Spangle sat, but was up again in two seconds.

"At least she's got Yap curious," said Neil. The Yorkie had crept to the door of his pen to see what the fuss was about. Ludo plodded to the mesh and pushed her nose against it. Yap's ears lifted a little, and he sniffed at her.

"That's the first good sign out of him yet," said Neil. "Maybe he'll come now."

Reluctantly, Yap joined them on their walk around the exercise field. Neil and Emily wanted to keep up a brisk pace against the chill of the frosty morning, but Ludo took her time and Neil noticed that Yap stayed close to her all the time.

"He might be cold," suggested Emily. "His coat's so thin."

"Spangle's happy," said Neil, watching her. She bounded ahead, stopped, raced back to him, then darted away again. In no time she found a large patch of mud and had a good roll before they could stop her. As Emily said, it was a good thing their mom and dad were used to a lot of washing. Spangle managed to share the mud very generously on the way back to the rescue center.

Back in his pen, Yap scuttled into a corner, refusing water and turning his head away from the biscuit Neil offered him. Neil stayed as long as he could, stroking Yap and talking to him, but nothing lifted the dog's misery. There were other dogs to be walked and homework to be done, and at last Neil had to leave him.

"I hope he settles down," said Neil to Emily. "It's terrible to see him like this."

"At last! I'm starving!" said Neil a few hours later, when Bob called upstairs to say that lunch was ready. He pushed his unfinished homework aside and ran to the kitchen. Bob gave the gravy a quick last stir as Carole lifted a tray of roast potatoes from the oven.

"Now," said Bob, as they sat down, "who likes house-work?"

Groans of disgust rose from all around the table.

"Terri called," Bob said. "She's been to see Mrs. Lumley. She still won't agree to part with any of her dogs, so Terri just has to keep on trying."

"Huh!" said Neil dramatically and stuffed a roast potato into his mouth.

"However, she *has* agreed to let a team of cleaner-uppers into the house. I offered to help. We can make it clean and comfortable for when she comes back, though the hospital won't say when that will be. And we can clean up the yard a little, too. That way, the neighbors won't have so much to complain about."

Emily reached for a pencil and an old envelope. "Should I work out a housework assignment chart?" she said helpfully.

"Bossy," muttered Neil.

"We'll do what we can," said Carole. "If there's any laundry to be done, I can do it here. But," she warned, "if she insists on having all the dogs back in the house, it will be too much for her to deal with. We can't help her out indefinitely."

"And that could spell trouble," added Bob.

CHAPTER FIVE

The whole family helped to clean Mrs. Lumley's house after school on Monday, though it was hard to know where to start. Emily opened windows to rid the house of its stale, doggy smell. There was the yard to be cleaned, well-chewed toys to be put away, and thick layers of dog hairs to be vacuumed from fraying carpets. There wasn't much they could do about the torn chair coverings and scratched doors.

After they had gone home and eaten, Carole went to the hospital to visit Maude Lumley. She left strict instructions about homework, and Neil sat at the table with his magazine article in front of him. He just couldn't get it right. Occasionally, he would crumple up a used sheet of paper and aim it at the wastepaper basket. Jake thought this was a great game, pouncing on every ball of paper with a noise that was meant to be a savage growl but was something like the whirr of a sewing machine. At least, thought Neil, somebody's enjoying this.

Sitting opposite him at the table, Emily had organized all her work into neat little piles. Pictures, maps, and diagrams were sorted into groups while she tried to put her school wildlife project together. Sarah tried to help by sorting out pictures but only managed to mix everything up.

"Oh, Sarah!" cried Emily at last. "Why don't you go and play with Fudge?"

Sarah pouted. "I'm only trying to help," she said.

Neil threw another sheet at the bin as Carole walked in. A draft of icy-cold air swept in with her as the door opened and shut. Jake ran over to be played with.

"How's Mrs. Lumley?" asked Emily.

Carole flopped onto a chair and patted Jake.

"Maude will be in the hospital for another week," she said. "It's not just her arm that's the problem. She's run down, anemic, and malnourished."

"She's probably better than the dogs," Neil muttered. He felt he shouldn't have said that, but he couldn't help it.

"You don't know that, Neil!" Carole's voice was so sharp that he flushed with shock. "She's looked after her dogs better than she's looked after herself. I think you should go to see her. They've been able to contact her older sister in Eastbourne. She's coming up this week. Hopefully, she'll take charge of the house, Maude, and everything else."

"That's all right, then," said Emily.

"I don't know. Maude didn't seem very pleased to hear her sister was coming."

"She's probably a bossy big sister," said Sarah. "Like mine." And she left the room with her nose in the air, nearly tripping over Jake. Neil and Emily stifled their giggles as they bent their heads over their homework, but Carole looked thoughtful. "Sarah could be right about that," she said.

Mike Turner came by on Tuesday, after his evening appointments, to drop off the last of Mrs. Lumley's dogs — Pippin and the puppy — and to check up on the others. Neil was already in Yap's pen, talking to him and offering him dog treats as the others toured the kennel. Mike examined Ludo first, running his hand over her joints, then watching the way she moved as she ambled toward him.

"She seems to be in less pain," he said as he bent down to pat her. "We'll see some improvement in her mobility soon. But she'll have to stay on this treatment. If she stops, she'll stiffen up again. How's the yappy Yorkie?"

Neil carried the miserable little terrier over to him. Mike's face creased into a frown. "Not too good, is he? Hasn't he found his appetite?"

"He's hardly eaten anything," Neil replied. "Just about enough to keep himself alive. I've tried talking to him, offering treats, lots of attention — he's just missing his home and Mrs. Lumley. He brightens up a bit when he goes for walks, but even then he wants to be close to Ludo. He might be happier if he shared her pen. I know we don't normally do it, but . . ."

"It might be the best thing, in this case," said Bob. "We do it for Sugar and Spice." The mention of Mrs. Jepsons's spoiled little terriers made Neil make a face.

"Anything that might get Yap eating and enjoying life is a good move," said Mike. "He really wants Mrs. Lumley, but Ludo is the next best thing."

Neil put Yap down while he opened the door of Ludo's pen and watched her amble inside. Yap followed her in. He sniffed at her dish and lapped up some water. Looking to see where Ludo had gone, he followed her to her bed and pawed at it inquisitively.

"It'll work, I think," said Mike. "How's Spangle?"

"Open the pen and stand back," said Bob. "Kate's started doing some basic obedience on her daily walks, but it's going to be a long job."

Spangle, having heard their voices, was already leaping up at the mesh hopefully and tumbled out of the door as soon as it was opened. She hurled herself at Bob, tried to greet Mike in midair, fell over, picked herself up, and had a good shake. Then she sneezed.

"Sit!" ordered Neil. The spaniel sat. "Good girl!" Neil smiled. "Believe it or not, she's better than she was. But she's got ants in her pants and likes a nice muddy puddle when she goes for a walk." By now, the dog had bounced up again. "Spangle, sit! Stay! She won't stay in one place for a second."

"Still chewing things?" asked Mike. Neil held up the tattered remnants of her bedding.

"I tried some of that stuff for getting them off chewing," said Neil, "but it hasn't worked. Maybe I didn't use enough?"

"No, don't worry," said Mike. "I suspect Maude has tried it before and Spangle is used to it."

"Do you think she might just calm down, when she gets used to us?"

"Possibly. She's gone from a home with a lot of stressed dogs to a strange environment. But if we don't do anything, you're going to have a bedding shortage soon!" Mike rubbed his chin, looked at Spangle's eager eyes, and thought for a moment. "Do you have any oil of cloves?"

"Never heard of it." Neil looked puzzled.

"It's an old-fashioned toothache remedy," said Bob.

"It is," said Mike. "It has a strong taste and dogs don't like it. My father used it." Mike patted the dog and she rubbed affectionately against his leg, leaving a spattering of white hairs. "How Maude Lumley coped with this bundle of fur, I don't know. Is Maude OK?"

"A little better," said Bob. "Carole tells me she's missing her dogs."

"Yeah, right!" mumbled Neil.

"Emily and Neil are going to see her tonight," said Bob. "I'm sure they'll fill her in on how everybody is doing!"

Neil scowled and moved along the row of pens to say hello to the rest of Maude Lumley's dogs.

At six o'clock that evening, Neil and Emily walked to the hospital, Emily carrying the basket of fruit from their parents that Neil refused to be seen with.

The hospital was situated on the approach to Compton, and it was a long, cold walk from the kennel. The building seemed unnaturally bright and warm as they looked for Ward 11.

"Children aren't usually allowed to visit without an adult," said a busy nurse. "But if you're Mrs. Parker's two, that's all right. She asked if you could come in. Don't talk too much and tire Mrs. Lumley out, OK?"

Neil and Emily followed the nurse to the second floor and stopped at the double door outside the ward.

The nurse looked at them again. "She needs lots of rest, and peace and quiet. You'll find her in the bed at the end on the left."

"I still don't know what to say to her," said Neil as they entered the ward. "You'll have to do the talking, Em." He looked uneasily down the room along the rows of beds and patients. "I can't even remember what she looks like."

Emily scanned the rows of beds. "That's her!" she said confidently. She was already walking to a bed where a frail, thin woman sat propped up on pillows. She wore a nightgown that looked too big for her.

"But she's tiny!" whispered Neil.

The woman waved with her left hand, and Neil saw that the other was set in plaster.

Reluctantly, Neil trudged after Emily, standing back as Mrs. Lumley thanked them for the fruit. The thought of the neglected dogs kept bothering him, and he still felt hostile.

"Find somewhere to sit, dears," she said. But while Emily perched on a stool, Neil stayed on his feet. This was bad enough without being called "dear." He hoped nobody had heard.

Mrs. Lumley beamed at him. "You've been looking after my dogs, haven't you?" she said. "It's very kind of you. Would you like some of this lovely fruit?"

Neil shook his head.

"It's a long time since I had anything so nice," she said happily. She certainly looked very thin and pale. There were flea bites on her arms.

Perhaps his mother had been right. It looked like Maude had struggled to do her best for her dogs.

"How are my dogs?" she asked eagerly. Neil found himself warming to his favorite subject, telling her all about King Street, reassuring her that the dogs were all eating well and being exercised. "Yap's a bit homesick," he said, "but Ludo and I look after him." He explained about Yap moving into Ludo's pen. "Mike's treated all their . . . um . . . infections."

"Oh, dear," she said, looking distressed. "I was going to take them to Mike as soon as I could afford it. The winter bills were so high this year, I had to put it off. And the cost of feeding them all! I needed a new insecticide spray, too, and I wanted Pippin's paw looked at. But it's difficult on a pension."

"It must be," said Emily. "Well, we've got them all in shape now. Spangle's a bit of a chewer, isn't she?"

Maude sighed. "I hope she isn't being a nuisance.

She goes through phases when she chews things. I think that's why her first owners abandoned her. She was only a puppy, and puppies do chew things, don't they? It's only natural."

"Where did you get Ludo from?" asked Emily.

Maude closed her eyes and thought. "Ludo must have been about six months old when she was abandoned on one of the country roads. You wouldn't think it, would you? A pedigree puppy, and with a lovely nature."

"Sam was abandoned by a railway line when we found him," said Neil. "He's my Border collie."

Maude understood. "It's terrible, isn't it? How people can be so cruel. Somebody just got tired of poor Ludo. They'd just tied a note with her name onto her collar and left her. It's wicked! She used to howl in the night. Perhaps that's why they didn't want her. But she was as good as gold when I let her sleep in my bedroom."

Neil couldn't help smiling.

"And Pippin," she went on, "he was a stray. Sean belonged to an old friend of mine who died two years ago, so of course I took him in at once."

"He must take a lot of feeding and exercising," said Neil.

"I think that's why nobody else offered to take him," said Maude. "And really, he isn't particular about what he eats, so long as he does eat. He can't help being such a big dog. Oh, I am glad he's with you. I know I had too many, but, you see, people got to know that I was a doggy sort of person. That little puppy . . ."

Her eyes filled with tears. She took a tissue from a box on the bedside table, dabbed her eyes, and blew her nose before she could go on.

"He was pushed under my gate, only two weeks ago," she said, "in an old cardboard box, with a bit of torn-up newspaper." She looked at Neil, and he saw his anger reflected in her eyes. "How can people do that? I was going to take him to Terri, but I simply hadn't gotten around to it."

The nurse was hovering over them.

"Are you all right, Maude? I hope you're not getting upset." She frowned at Neil. "I think it's time to go."

"Thank you so much for coming," said Mrs. Lumley. "I've enjoyed this. Oh, I wish I could see my dogs again. Only for a moment. I'm sure they're having the best of care. I just wish I could see them."

She clutched Neil's hand, and he squeezed it back briefly.

Maybe Mrs. Lumley wasn't the person he'd thought she was after all.

"But I still think she shouldn't have let the dogs get into such a terrible state," Neil said later that evening, as he recounted their visit to the rest of the family. "I do think she cares, though. She did her best. I can see that, now," he ended, thoughtfully.

"It's a tragic story," muttered Carole.

"She won't be happy till she sees them," said Emily. "Then she'll see for herself that they're doing fine."

Sarah was practicing her ballet exercises in the middle of the room. "She could see them through a window," she remarked.

Neil looked up. "Squirt, you're brilliant!" he said.

"I know," said Sarah with a little shrug.

"I can just see it," chuckled Bob. "Eight dogs lined up at the hospital window, noses pressed up at the glass. Mrs. Lumley looking out at them!"

Sarah rolled over on the floor, laughing. Jake joined in, so that he and Sarah became a six-legged tangle on the floor.

Neil was thinking things out. "There's a path that runs along the back of the hospital, isn't there? It joins on to the ridgeway, but part of it runs along the other side of the parking lot. If we walked the dogs along there, she could see them from her window. We'd need a prearranged time, though, so she'd know when to look out."

"Hold on," said Carole. "Isn't her room on the second floor? And won't it be dark?"

"The path is very close to the hospital building," said Emily, joining in. "There are lights — she'll still be able to see them!"

"Fair enough," agreed Carole. "It does sound like a good idea, if it can stop Maude from fretting so much. But you can't take eight dogs!"

"Of course not," said Neil. "We'll just take the Three Musketeers!"

"That reminds me," said Bob. "You two come with me to the rescue center. There's something you should see."

They followed him to Yap's pen. It had been cleared and washed down and was ready for the next occupant. In the adjoining pen, there were two empty feeding dishes and two bowls of water, side by side.

"He ate every scrap," said Bob, "and look at him now."

Ludo lay sprawling in her sleep, paws twitching. Yap was curled up against her, one paw rested on her flank, his head nestled against her as he slept.

"We can stop worrying about him," said Bob. "His owner may be fretting, but he isn't."

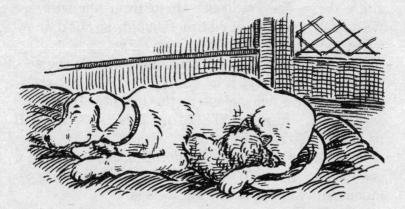

CHAPTER SIX

The next evening, Ludo, Spangle, and Yap seemed puzzled to be taken beyond the exercise field and given a much longer walk than usual. The wind was cold as they walked along the path that led behind the hospital. Neil and Emily walked with hunched shoulders and their heads down. A wooden fence with a gate separated the path from the hospital parking lot. Neil took up his place at the gate, Ludo and Yap sitting obediently beside him as he scanned the row of lit windows on the second floor. Spangle fidgeted on the leash and put her paws up on the gate.

Neil looked at his watch. "It's six o'clock now. I hope she remembers what Mom told her."

"There she is," said Emily, pointing up to a shape in one of the nearest windows.

Mrs. Lumley, a white-haired figure wrapped in a dressing gown, stood peering out, anxiously scanning the path. Then, as she caught sight of the three dogs, her face was transformed with a smile of such love and delight that Neil was amazed.

Their chilly walk had been worthwhile just to see the look on her face.

But a fine drizzle was falling. "Home now, Ludo," Neil said. Ludo's arthritis could get worse if she became cold and wet. Neil and Emily gave one last wave toward the window and led the dogs away. When they were almost out of sight of the hospital, Neil turned and looked again.

She was still there.

She leaned forward, her cheek pressed to the window, straining for the very last glimpse of her Musketeers. Neil waved once more and saw her wave back.

There was no chance of a dog walk the next day. The rain set in early and didn't stop. Neil and Emily didn't mind getting wet, but it wasn't ideal weather for the dogs, especially Ludo.

It was Friday when they managed to walk to the hospital again.

"Put your boots on," said Bob. "With any luck, you'll tire Spangle out. That path will be muddy after all the rain."

"So will Spangle," Emily pointed out as she pulled on her waterproof jacket. It didn't seem possible to keep Spangle out of the mud for long.

"See you later," said Bob.

Emily picked up Yap and Ludo at the rescue center, while Neil headed for Spangle's pen. When she saw that he was carrying a leash, she jumped up and playfully pawed at his sweatshirt.

Neil decided to try out one of his father's favorite methods of making a dog wait patiently to have the leash put on.

He stood still, put the leash behind his back, and waited. Spangle, puzzled, stopped jumping up and sat down, tipping her head to one side. When the leash appeared again she bounced and barked with excitement, but again, Neil hid it.

"Sit," he ordered. "Stay!" It took a couple more attempts at the same procedure, but at last Spangle seemed to get the idea and waited patiently for Neil to fasten on her leash. She was restless, longing for a good run and beating her tail on the floor, but she sat as quietly as she could. He could see she was trying very hard to behave herself.

After a few obedience lessons she still pulled on the leash, but at least she didn't pull quite as hard as before.

The long walk settled her down a bit, too. She couldn't resist putting her nose into a hedge and getting twigs and burrs in her ears, and there was a lot of mud around, but she was as clean as could be hoped for when they reached the gate at the back of the hospital.

Ludo and Yap waited patiently with Emily for the gate to be opened, but Spangle didn't. She put both paws on the fence to take a good look around. Neil saw Mrs. Lumley's face break into a broad smile at one of the windows up above. Neil and Emily led them forward, so they could be seen more clearly.

"Come on, then," Neil said at last. But Spangle, with a low growl rolling in her throat, stopped. Her eyes were fixed on something. Neil followed her gaze.

An orange cat was stepping daintily around a gleaming car. It rubbed its face lazily against the hubcap, then turned and disappeared underneath the car.

"Come on, Spangle," said Neil, with a sharp tug on the leash. He had never seen her with a cat, and he didn't want to now.

But it was too late. The cat crept out on the other side of the car and, as Spangle saw the cat, the cat saw Spangle. Its spine arched and bristled, and it bared its teeth and hissed.

Neil pulled back hard on the leash, but in an immense jerk in the opposite direction Spangle wrenched free and tore recklessly after the cat. Her ears were flapping, and the dog leash flailed in the air behind her amidst a fury of barking.

Alarmed by the sudden noise, indignant nurses and curious patients appeared at almost every window of the hospital.

Neil raced across the lot as a car turned a corner and swerved wildly around Spangle. Unhurt, the dog vanished from view as the car came to a halt in a parking spot marked CONSULTANT. A tall, angry woman with a black briefcase got out and slammed the door.

"Can't you control your dog?" she snapped. "You're lucky I'm in a hurry." And she ran to the nearest entrance, nearly colliding with a tall man who then stormed up to Neil. The badge on his lapel read HOSPITAL ADMINISTRATOR.

"Are you the cause of all this commotion?" he demanded. "Patients could be upset by all that barking, and now I find your dog nearly causing an accident. That lady is a consulting surgeon, and she's just been called in to do an emergency operation. She could have crashed her car because of your dog."

"I'm sorry," said Neil, but he knew the apology sounded lame. He tried to explain. "It isn't my dog. I'm just walking her for Mrs. Lumley . . . she's in the hospital . . . but Spangle saw a cat . . . and she just took off — I mean, the dog, not Mrs. Lumley. I'm really sorry. I tried, but I couldn't hold her." He hoped the man would let him go now. The longer this took, the farther away Spangle would go. "Please can I go to find her? If the cat runs across a main road . . ."

"Neil, hurry!" shouted Emily from somewhere behind him, still holding on to Yap and Ludo.

"Yes, go on, then." The man sounded less threatening than before. "And if the dog's uncontrollable, please don't bring it back around here!"

Neil ran in what he hoped was the right direction, calling Spangle's name, but there was no trace of her. Emily followed, but it was impossible to run with Ludo and Yap. At the main road, Neil stopped to ask the people waiting at the bus stop if she had passed that way, but nobody had seen her.

"I suppose she'll head for home," said Emily, catching up with him. "But where does she think home is? King Street or Windsor Drive?"

"Windsor Drive, I would think," said Neil. "If she could find her way. It's not that far. We'd better get moving."

"We won't look too good if we turn up at home without her," said Emily. "Come on, Ludo, Yap. Let's find your friend."

They arrived at Windsor Drive flushed from the cold and desperate for a rest. Their efforts were rewarded: Spangle sat on the doorstep of number 24,

barking and pawing hopefully at the scratched front door.

"Phew!" Emily breathed a sigh of relief and flopped down on the steps beside her with Ludo and Yap.

"Quiet! Down! There's a good girl," said Neil, catching hold of the excited spaniel's leash. He gave the runaway dog a reassuring pat. "Come on, Spangle, let's get you back to King Street before —"

"Ssh!" said Emily. "There's someone in the house!"

The front door opened suddenly. In the light of the hallway stood a smartly dressed woman.

"Oh!" said Neil. Thinking quickly, he remembered his mom saying something about Maude having a sister. "You must be Mrs. Lumley's sister."

"No, I'm the Environmental Health Officer," she said briskly. "If you want Mrs. Jennings, she's in the house." As she hurried away, another woman emerged from the hallway and stood on the doorstep. She was neat and gray-haired, with a firm step and a stern expression. She didn't seem at all pleased to see them and looked coldly down at Spangle.

"Sit!" she ordered.

Spangle sat.

The woman regarded Neil and Emily as if she'd like to do the same with them.

"We're Emily and Neil Parker," explained Emily. "We're from King Street Kennels."

"I am Mrs. Jennings," she said. "My sister is not at home."

Neil explained how they came to be on her doorstep with a muddy spaniel who never stayed "sat" for very long.

"I'm sure you've been very helpful," said Mrs. Jennings, but she still sounded like a teacher giving them a lecture. "I know you and your family have done a lot to help Maude. But I'll take over now, thank you. This house is to be sold, and all the dogs will have to be rehoused, whether Maude likes it or not. She simply can't deal with them anymore. I expect I'll be in touch with your parents about that."

"Oh, poor Mrs. Lumley!" cried Emily. Ludo and Yap both whined as if they had understood what their owner's sister had just said.

Mrs. Jennings glared at them. "It has to be done. Mr. Crosby has been telling me what Maude's dogs have been up to recently. Barking at all hours, running off, and frightening frail old people in the street. And the neighbors here take great care of their gardens; they don't take kindly to an army of dogs digging up the flowerbeds!"

"I'm sure they didn't mean it," mumbled Neil, ruffling Spangle's ears.

"It's not just that," continued Mrs. Jennings. "This house has been left to crumble, and if Maude had stayed here much longer it would have collapsed around her ears. It won't bring in half of what it's worth when we sell it."

"But please, Mrs. Lumley *needs* to have a dog — even just one dog!" pleaded Emily. She looked at Ludo and Yap, who also seemed to be listening intently.

"I can't talk about this now," said Mrs. Jennings. "I have things to do. I think you should go. Surely it's past your bedtime! Good-bye."

"Good-bye," Emily stammered as the door closed in front of them.

"Come on," said Neil, looking down at the dogs. In low spirits, they set off for home. Even Spangle seemed dejected.

"That's Mr. Crosby," said Emily as they walked down Windsor Drive. Mr. Crosby was on a doorstep, with a clipboard in his hand. On the other side of the road, his wife was also carrying a clipboard as she walked down a garden path.

"Wonder what they're up to?" said Neil. "She's coming this way."

Mrs. Crosby saw them as they came near. She looked nervously at Spangle and shrank away as the dog came near.

"She won't hurt you," said Emily. Neil was keeping Spangle on a short leash so she couldn't jump up, but Mrs. Crosby still eyed her anxiously.

"She's a good dog, really," began Neil. "They all are." But Mr. Crosby had seen them and was running across the road to them.

"I'll deal with this, Muriel," he insisted. "You'd better keep those dogs away from Muriel, understand? And you needn't think they're coming back here. I vowed that if one more dog came to that house, I'd take action, and that's what I'm doing. The police and Environmental Health won't do anything, so I will."

"They're coming home with us!" protested Emily, standing between Mr. Crosby and the three dogs protectively.

But Mr. Crosby had taken his wife by the arm and was hurrying her away.

"Did you get a good look at the clipboard?" asked Neil as he and Emily went on their way.

"Yes, it looked like a petition. I spotted the word 'nuisance' and Mrs. Lumley's address. It looks as if they're ganging up against her."

"What can they do about her, though?" said Neil. "Make her leave her home? Stop her from keeping dogs?"

"I don't know," said Emily, "but there were a lot of names on that petition."

Neil pulled Spangle closer and patted her. "Never mind, Spangle," he said. "I know trouble seems to follow you, but it really isn't your fault. And somehow, we'll get you and Mrs. Lumley together again."

CHAPTER SEVEN

Neil and Emily reached home cold, tired, and dejected, but the sight of the white SPCA van brightened them up.

"Terri's here!" said Emily, as Carole came out to meet them.

"You look frozen," she said. "You've been gone a long time. Here, give me the dogs, I'll take them and settle them down. At least I won't have to give Spangle new bedding again. She hasn't eaten the last one yet. Terri's in the kitchen."

Jake's yaps of excitement at seeing Neil and Sam's wagging tail were the nicest things that had happened to Neil all day. Neil petted Sam with one hand and Jake with the other. Bob had just boiled water

in the kettle, so there was soon a hot drink for everyone.

"Terri's got good news," said Bob.

Neil looked up.

"Yes," said Terri. "Maude is coming home from the
hospital tomorrow. Even the doctors couldn't keep
her in for more than a week. She's so determined!"

"That's great news," said Emily.

"There's more," added Terri. "She's agreed to sign
most of the dogs over to the SPCA. I finally talked
her into it. So Pippin and the rest will come with me
to the SPCA kennel tomorrow until we can find them
good homes. We'll have them all neutered and spayed,
too, *before* they're rehoused. That makes for fewer
unwanted puppies in the future."

"Can she keep Spangle?" said Neil.

"She *insists* on keeping Spangle. And Yap. And
Ludo," sighed Terri. She glanced up at Bob, who was
chuckling softly. "Yes, I know. It may be too much for
her, but we had to compromise. I'll keep working
with her to make sure she can manage, and if she
can't care for them properly, I'll just have to insist.
But we have to let her try."

"We'll help," said Neil. "I thought at first she
shouldn't be allowed near a dog again, but she just
had too many. She really does care about them all.
She'll be so pleased to see them and I think she
should have a second chance."

Terri frowned. "Bob, are her dogs over their infections?"

"Just about." Bob scratched his beard. "We'll let them go as long as Mike pronounces them clear. He's due in the morning."

"If it's up to her sister, she won't have them at all," said Emily. "Mrs. Jennings is dead against it."

"Mrs. Jennings?" asked Bob. Neil and Emily looked guiltily at each other. They knew they couldn't put off telling them about Spangle's adventure at the hospital any longer. As Carole came in from the rescue center, they explained how they came to be on Mrs. Lumley's doorstep with Spangle.

"We're supposed to be responsible for other people's dogs," frowned Carole. "Incidents like that aren't acceptable. It's bad for the dogs and it's bad for King Street. What if Spangle had been knocked down on the road?"

"I know, Mom, I thought of that," said Neil. "I'm sorry."

"You should be," added Bob. "So, what did Mrs. Jennings say?"

Emily repeated what Mrs. Jennings had said. "And it would be terrible for Mrs. Lumley to lose her home and all her dogs," she finished.

"The dogs are *our* concern," said Bob. "Mrs. Lumley and her sister have to sort out their own arguments. We can't get involved in other people's family affairs."

"It's not fair!" exploded Neil. "She needs her dogs! Her three special dogs! That's all she wants!"

"They'd go to good homes," Terri pointed out.

"They'll go to their *own* home," said Neil.

The following day was a Saturday. In the morning, Neil helped Terri put the SPCA dogs into the van for their departure from King Street. From large, loping Sean to the chubby puppy — nicknamed Pat — they all had smooth, shiny coats. Pippin walked beside Neil with barely a trace of a limp.

When they had gone, Neil began cleaning the empty pens. It was always hard to say good-bye to a dog, but if he worked hard, he wouldn't think about it too much.

Of the original eight dogs from Windsor Drive, only Spangle, Yap, and Ludo remained. Mike Turner came by just before lunch to check that the last three were fit enough to leave, too.

"You've done a wonderful job here, Neil," he said. He watched Yap trotting at Neil's heel in the court-yard. "And Ludo will be fine if she stays on her med-ication. There's a world of difference in the way she moves. As for Spangle, look at her! Sitting there, good as gold! What's happened to her?"

"Oh, she still has her moments," said Bob, casting a suspicious eye toward the spaniel sitting on her haunches on the edge of the square. "Kate and Neil

have helped her to settle down a lot, and the oil of cloves seems to have worked. She's lost her chewing habit. But I wouldn't like to see her with a cat — not after her last performance. I'll take them home this afternoon. Neil, do you want to come along?"

"But Mrs. Jennings doesn't want them," Neil reminded him. "What can we do about that?"

"I've told you, that isn't our problem. Mrs. Lumley wants her dogs back. That's all there is to it. How she and her sister sort out their arguments is none of our business."

*　　*　　*

After lunch Neil brushed Yap's coat in the workroom until it gleamed. Yap shrank away at first but gradually found he enjoyed being groomed, rubbing his face against the brush.

Ludo loved to be brushed, pawing at Neil to start again if he paused.

Spangle thought it was a great game to see who could catch the brush and spent her own grooming session twisting around to try and snatch it out of Neil's hand. She looked presentable when it was over, but Neil's mistake was to groom her before her walk. As soon as she reached the field, she found a patch of mud and had a good roll.

"The idea is to take her back smelling better than she did in the first place," said Bob when he inspected Neil's grooming exercise. "Neil, take her and give her a quick wash."

"Won't that make her shed everywhere?" said Neil.

"I'm afraid so, but it can't be helped," said Bob.

By the time Bob, Neil, and Emily arrived at Windsor Drive, Spangle had left white hair all over the van and everybody in it.

"Mrs. Jennings must be a woman who gets things done," Bob remarked as they parked outside the house. The windows were open, and clean curtains wafted in the breeze. Mrs. Jennings's shiny car was parked outside and the dogs sniffed at it with keen interest.

"Don't you dare, Yap," said Bob. "I don't think Mrs.

Jennings would see the funny side of her car being Yap's toilet. She seems to like everything in order."

In spite of the chilly afternoon, the front door was open. Through it came the high and snappy notes of two angry voices.

"We seem to have come at a bad time," Bob said softly. He tentatively rang the doorbell. "But we can't help that."

Maude Lumley came to the door moments later, and the difference in her amazed Neil. Her clothes were neat and clean, her hair softly brushed, and she walked with a firm step. She looked younger, too, and had color in her face. She appeared at first with a tight frown on her face, which changed into a beaming smile as she saw her dogs. Spangle and Yap bounded to her, barking with joy, and Ludo followed as quickly as she could.

"My best friends! Come in! Yap! Spangle! Ludo, I've missed you!"

"Down, Spangle!" called Bob, raising his voice over the barking of the dogs. "Don't let her jump up at your bad arm, Maude. Careful she doesn't knock you over. Spangle, be quiet!"

Mrs. Lumley looked up from the jumble of dogs jostling to greet her. "Ludo looks so much better. What have you done with her? Spangle, have you had a bath?"

"Hello, Mrs. Jennings!" said Emily brightly as Mrs.

Lumley's sister walked down the hall toward them without so much as a smile. Bob looked up and reached out his hand.

"Mrs. Jennings? I'm Bob Parker, from King Street Kennels."

"Yes, I see." She looked at her sister on her knees among the nuzzling, tail-wagging dogs and sighed. "You'd better come in. Does that spaniel always shed so much?"

"Oh, Val, what does it matter?" laughed Mrs. Lumley.

"When I've just cleaned every corner of this house and washed all the chair covers, it matters a great deal." She led the way into the living room, where the dogs ran about investigating the unfamiliar smells of insecticide and carpet cleaner. A bunch of flowers on a table gave the room a summery aroma despite the overcast sky outside.

"I was just pointing out to Maude," Val Jennings said, "that the dogs can only be here for a short time. Maude can hardly look after this house by herself, let alone three dogs. One, maybe, but not three."

"They're my dogs, Val!" snapped Mrs. Lumley. She sat down, and Ludo rested her head contentedly on her mistress's knee. Yap lay down across her feet. "Look at this! How can I send them away?"

"How can you do anything else? Oh, look, that spaniel's clawing at the hearthrug already!"

Neil called Spangle to him and sat on the floor beside her. He draped an arm over her flank. He wanted to keep her out of trouble.

"You know what will happen," Mrs. Jennings went on. "Do you want them to end up in the state they were in before the SPCA took them away?"

"That isn't fair! It wasn't like that!" cried Mrs. Lumley tearfully.

"I think we'd better go," said Bob, and, with Neil and Emily, moved toward the door.

"Please don't!" said Mrs. Lumley. "She's bullying me like she always has. She treats me like an idiot!"

"This is really none of our business," said Bob.

"I hope you will stay," said Mrs. Jennings. "We do need to discuss the future of the dogs."

Maude Lumley shook her head.

"Yes, Maude, we do," persisted Mrs. Jennings.

"I don't see why," moaned Mrs. Lumley. "They're *my* dogs." She picked up Yap and held him closely.

"But the house was left to *both* of us. I have a half-share in this house, and the value of it has gone down by thousands because *you* neglected it so much. I'm not surprised the neighbors have complained." Mrs. Jennings sighed. "It's not just the animals, Maude. You can't afford to keep a house this size. You won't be sensible, so I'll have to insist. Sell it and buy a little modern apartment. Perhaps you could take one quiet little dog."

"But I can't separate these dogs!" Mrs. Lumley

protested. "Val, you don't understand anything at all. You're doing what you've always done — interfering. Just because you're older than I am, you always think you know best."

Neil sat still with Spangle. He looked from one angry woman to the other. They were both on their feet now, hands clenched, eyes wide and glaring.

"And what would have happened if I hadn't interfered?" demanded Mrs. Jennings. "You'd still be in the hospital because there'd be nobody here to look after you, and this house would be totally neglected." She softened her tone a little. "And *all* your dogs would have been re-homed." She glanced at Bob. "I'm very grateful for all you and your family have done here, Mr. Parker, but she can't expect you all to go on running after her."

Neil tried to point out that they didn't mind, but nobody listened.

Val Jennings's voice rose as she turned on her sister again. "And you can't expect it of me, Maude, either!"

"I don't expect anything of you!" Mrs. Lumley replied defensively.

"Nonsense, Maude! I always have to take care of you! I've left my own home, in the middle of winter, to come here and get this — this *mess* — straightened out, and all I get from you is a lot of bleating about dogs!"

"You never did like dogs, Val, that's why you don't

understand." Mrs. Lumley turned to the Parkers. "You ought to know that my sister was bitten by a sheepdog when she was a little girl. She's never liked dogs since."

"Maude, will you stop talking nonsense? Oh, I give up. I may as well go straight home to Eastbourne. If you would only listen, Maude . . ."

"Listen!" shouted Emily. There was instant silence, and everyone stared at her.

Emily turned deep red. "I meant, 'Listen, the doorbell's ringing,'" she said. The argument had become so loud and angry, nobody else had heard it. But Mr. Crosby, tired of ringing and waiting on the step, had already invited himself in and stood scowling in the living room doorway. Mrs. Lumley turned to meet him as Bob quieted the barking dogs.

"Mrs. Lumley," he said, in a low, cold voice. "I see those dogs are back. Three of them! I've already called the Environmental Health Officer to warn her that all this trouble is starting again. The neighbors have all agreed. We've had enough of your noisy, dangerous dogs. I've promised I won't rest while there's a dog left in this house!"

"Excuse me!" With a firm, disapproving voice, Mrs. Jennings tilted up her chin and looked him in the eyes. There was silence. She took a step forward. "Good afternoon, Mr. Crosby. You have not asked how my sister is, you have not welcomed her home. She is considerably better, but she is in no state

to be upset by an intruder in her home. Yes, Mr. Crosby, you are an intruder. You barged in here without permission and without consideration for anyone."

"Wow!" whispered Emily to Neil.

All this reminded Neil of Sheba, a dog they had once helped at King Street. Tiny as she was, she had reduced Ben, Julie Barker's enormous English Sheepdog, into timid submission. He was watching something like it now.

Mr. Crosby no longer looked so sure of himself. He moved away from Mrs. Jennings. "I'm sorry," he said nervously, "but we can't have this sort of situation. It's very distressing."

"Mr. Crosby, you see before you a clean house and a lady who has just been sent home from the hospital. I hope you don't find that distressing."

"No, but, you know," said Mr. Crosby, struggling, "the dogs . . ."

"The dogs are perfectly under control," said Bob quietly. Neil held on tightly to Spangle, patting her gently.

"And now I think you should leave, Mr. Crosby," said Mrs. Jennings. "My sister is tired."

She advanced toward him, and he had no choice but to head for the front door. She shut it very firmly.

Neil and Emily broke into applause as she returned, and Mrs. Lumley sat down weakly.

"You needn't think I'm turning soft," snapped Val Jennings. "I haven't changed my mind about anything. But I'll sort out this house — and the dogs, *and* you, Maude — myself. And no bullying neighbors are going to get in my way!"

CHAPTER EIGHT

The Parkers left as soon as they could, and for two days there was no news from the Lumley household. This, they hoped, was a good sign.

On Monday evening, as Bob and Carole cleared the kitchen table, Neil, slowly and reluctantly, got out his books to do some homework. "I wonder how Mrs. Lumley's doing?" he said.

"You mean, 'How are the dogs?'" said Carole. "I'm sure they're fine. I don't suppose this is just a way of putting off your homework, is it, Neil?"

"Neil put off his homework?" said Bob. "What homework do you have, Neil?"

"My magazine thing," he admitted.

"Neil, haven't you finished that yet?" asked Carole.

"No, but I've started it a million times. I was going

to write a piece about Terri's work. Then I thought I'd write something about neglected dogs, but . . ."

"But what?" asked Carole, as he hesitated.

"But it's turning out differently. I want to write about Mrs. Lumley and her dogs, and how nobody understands her. But there's so much to say, I don't know how I'll ever finish it."

"Try, Neil. I'm sure it'll be an excellent article when it's done," Carole encouraged him. She removed a heap of books from a chair and sat down beside him. "You want to get it published, don't you?"

"Yes," he grumbled, then jumped to his feet. "Mom, Jake's scratching at the door. I'd better take him out."

Neil tried to sort out his ideas as he stood on the back step, watching Jake. The puppy scurried around the garden, fighting with a ball and shaking bits of stick. Neil was calling him in when Sarah ran into the kitchen, pigtails flying.

"Neil! Emily! Spangle's on television!" she cried.

Neil and Emily ran to the next room, followed by Carole.

They were just in time to see a shot of Spangle, a little muddy and with bits of dead leaf in her ears, but happy and healthy, playing with a ball in Mrs. Lumley's garden. Then the camera turned to a well-known face.

"Who's that?" asked Carole.

"Mr. Crosby," said Neil. "The nosiest neighbor in Compton!"

"Does he always look so angry?"

"All of us in this street have been very patient," Mr. Crosby was saying to the camera, "but we can't tolerate this anymore! Mrs. Lumley has only just come home and she's got three dogs in there already. In no time at all we'll be back to the smells and the noise and frail old people afraid to walk down the street for fear of a dog knocking them over. The dogs are at risk, too. I heard a dog yelping today. I've told the SPCA."

"I hate Mr. Crosby," said Emily.

"That's enough," said Carole. Bob came in, with Jake at his heels.

"It's not fair to neighbors who've spent a lot of money on their houses," Mr. Crosby went on. "On this street, we take pride in our homes. We've added new features, we've built on porches and green-houses."

He listed the glories of Windsor Drive as the screen showed pictures of smart white greenhouses, porches with hanging baskets, posh gardens, pools, and mini-waterfalls.

"We spend all this money on our houses," he continued, "but if we want to sell them, we can't get a reasonable price. Who wants to live next to that? Look at it!"

The camera showed the outside of Mrs. Lumley's house with its peeling paint and patchy yard. The front door was scratched from the pawing of dogs over the years. Even after all the work they had done, it looked shabby on the outside when compared with all the others.

"That's so unfair," protested Neil. "It makes it look as if he's right about everything and that Mrs. Lumley is a villain."

"Remember how you felt, Neil, when you first went to the house?" said Bob. "Then *you* were the one who thought she should be locked up. Now get back to your magazine article, and don't trip over Jake. He's just behind you."

"Good boy, Jake," said Neil, bending down to remove the puppy's front paws from his trousers. Then he thought of something. "Jake!" he repeated, and a smile spread across his face.

When Bob saw him again moments later, he was flipping through the telephone book.

"This will help with my magazine article," he said with a grin of triumph. "Honest!"

On Friday, when the next edition of the *Compton News* came out, Neil was up early. He had already set the table for breakfast and put the kettle on when Bob came downstairs.

"Morning, Dad!"

Puzzled, Bob looked from Neil to the table and back. "What's all this about?"

Neil beamed at him. "Cup of tea, Dad? I'll make some toast." It was important to get him into a good mood. Neil wasn't quite sure what he'd say when the newspapers arrived.

At the sound of the papers dropping through the mail slot, Neil hurried to get to them before Jake, who had been known to chew them up, on occasion. He put them on the table in front of Bob and waited for his father to notice the color picture on the front page of the *Compton News*.

"That's the Lumley Three!" he said. He glanced at Neil over the top of the paper, then read in silence while Neil sat and waited for what seemed a very, very long time. He wished someone else would come downstairs to ease the tension.

Bob finally lifted his eyes from the paper to look at Neil. Then he read aloud from the newspaper: "*Eleven-year-old Neil Parker of King Street Kennels told us, 'Mrs. Lumley really loves dogs. She couldn't manage eight of them, but three are no problem. The SPCA will help her to look after them. I should think the dog yelping was just Yap asking for a walk — he always makes that noise. And as for the house, there's nothing the matter with it. Dogs are more important than new porches.'*"

Bob placed the newspaper on the table and folded his large hands over it. "Unfortunately, Neil, not everyone on Windsor Drive would agree with you," he said.

"I had to do it, Dad. Somebody had to tell the other side of things — Mrs. Lumley's side."

"And that someone had to be you?" asked Bob as Carole strode into the kitchen. He pushed the paper toward her. "Neil, have you any idea of the harm you could have done? You've involved King Street in this issue now. As far as the press is concerned, we've taken one side against the other. The media can make what they want out of this. They can make Mrs. Lumley look like a crank."

"I only called Jake Fielding," said Neil. "He was really interested. Jake — our Jake — made me think about him." Jake Fielding was the photographer from the paper, and he had helped King Street Kennels out of many sticky situations.

"You should have kept your mouth shut, Jake," said Carole to the puppy.

"I suppose Jake Fielding is safe enough," said Bob. "But the same can't be said for any other reporters who might follow up on this story. Neil, I know you're concerned with the dogs, I know you mean well. And one day, your brain will catch up with your heart. Until then, leave the press to me and your mom."

"So if anyone calls up asking about Mrs. Lumley, or any of this," said Carole, "ask one of us. Don't try to deal with it yourself. Promise?"

"Promise."

"OK," said Bob. "Now go and take your dogs out before Sam scratches the door down."

"Thanks, Dad!" said Neil as he ran outside.

*　　*　　*

The local press did make the most of the story. The telephone seemed to ring continually over the weekend and for the rest of the week. Bob and Carole even began leaving the answering machine switched on so they could get on with running the kennel. When Bob did talk to reporters, it was only to tell them that the SPCA was monitoring the welfare of the dogs. His kind, bearded face appeared in papers and on local news shows. So did the discontented scowl of Mr. Crosby and other neighbors.

"They'll only dig up our gardens," said one. "It's all right while her sister is there, but she'll go when Mrs. Lumley's arm is better."

"Those dogs terrorize old people in the street," said another, and a third said that the market price of his house had gone down.

"It doesn't look too good for Maude," said Carole on Friday evening. "If I were her, I'd be worried. Neil, have you finished —"

"Your magazine article!" said Bob and Emily together and laughed.

Neil kept his gaze on the TV. "I need some photos before it's finished," he said. "I thought I'd go over tomorrow and ask Mrs. Lumley if I can take some pictures of the dogs."

"I'll come, too," said Emily. "I'd love to see the dogs again. And Mrs. Lumley. The way things are going, she needs all the friends she can get."

* * *

"You'd better come in," said Mrs. Lumley when they arrived on her doorstep the following morning. Her eyes were bloodshot, and she held a crumpled tissue in one quivering hand. Around her, the dogs barked and jumped in welcome and Yap, who had learned that Neil and Emily meant walks, started his excited yelping. Whatever was upsetting Mrs. Lumley, Neil thought, there was nothing the matter with the dogs.

"Be quiet, Yap! Down, Spangle!" she ordered. "Val will be back soon. She went shopping."

"Are you all right, Mrs. Lumley?" asked Emily, stroking Ludo's head as they followed Mrs. Lumley into the living room. "You're shaking! You'd better sit down."

Mrs. Lumley seated herself and lifted Yap onto her knees. "I'm just a little upset," she said. "It's about Sergeant Moorhead."

"He's been here?" asked Emily.

"He's a nice man, really," said Mrs. Lumley distractedly. "I suppose he was only doing his job."

"What did he want?" asked Neil, patting Ludo as she pawed at him.

"Well, I saw him coming out of Mr. Crosby's just a few minutes ago. I'm afraid Mr. Crosby must have complained again, and the sergeant went to get all the details. I might get a summons for the dogs making noise. They call it noise pollution, don't they? I'm so afraid." Mrs. Lumley's face was creased with worry. "I don't know where all this is going to end!" she went on. "This last week has been awful. I'm afraid to take the dogs out for walks."

Emily knelt at her feet. "The neighbors don't have anything to complain about, have they?" she asked.

"I'm afraid they're right about the house," admitted Mrs. Lumley, looking about her at the faded carpets and worn chair covers. "It's a bit shabby. I know the paintwork outside needs doing. There just hasn't been the money to spend on it — not with a lot of dogs to feed . . ."

"The police won't arrest you just because you haven't painted the front door!" said Emily, and Mrs. Lumley laughed weakly.

"And if they have been complaining about the dogs again," said Neil, "and if you do have to go to court, we'll speak for you. I'm sure my dad will stand up for you, too."

"Don't be silly, Neil." Emily glared at him. "Nobody's going to take Mrs. Lumley to court. Look, the dogs expect a walk because we're here." Yap had already placed himself hopefully at the front door, and Spangle was beginning to dart around in agitation.

"We can't disappoint them, then, can we?" said Neil. "Mrs. Lumley, can we walk the dogs for you?"

"Would you, dear? That would be so kind. They'd like that."

Emily wriggled to her feet, and the dogs led them hopefully to the front door, where leashes were hanging on coat hooks. Neil unhooked one, looked hard at Spangle, and hid it behind his back until she sat quietly, her head to one side and her tail thumping on the floor.

"Come on," Emily giggled. "And don't forget the camera. Ludo, Yap, you're with me. And," she added softly, "behave yourselves. You're all in enough trouble already, so don't go making any more."

"We'll have to go past the Crosbys' house," said Neil. "With any luck they'll see the dogs, clean and under control. Are you listening, Spangle? Behave!"

CHAPTER NINE

"**H**eel, Spangle!" said Neil, as they walked along the length of Windsor Drive with Maude Lumley's three dogs. "My heel, not Emily's, you silly thing." He laughed as the dog veered back toward him. "I don't believe this dog. She's a complete featherbrain, but she's fun."

"And I just love Ludo," said Emily. "She's so gentle. Yes, Yap, I love you, too."

In the woods, on the Compton side of the ridgeway, Neil and Emily unclipped the dogs' leashes to give them a long run. Spangle galloped away into the dark leaves. It was a dry, mild day, and the three dogs had their noses to the ground to sniff at all the strange and tempting scents in the seclusion of

the woods. Yap sped after Spangle, then found a
scent and busied himself scratching and snuffling
among tree roots. Even Ludo loped about, sniffing
suspiciously at a feather and sneezing when it tickled her nose.

"She's amazing," said Emily happily. "I can't believe how much better she is."

There was a commotion in the undergrowth, rust-
ling and flapping, and a thrush flew into the air. Yap,
very pleased with himself, turned sharply around,
snapped at it, and startled a blackbird as well.

"I thought you wanted photos," said Emily.

"I'll take some when we get back to the house,"
said Neil, who had forgotten all about them. "Yap's
found a trail. He must be after a rabbit or something. Oh, no — Spangle!"

There was nothing they could do. Spangle had found
just the sort of muddy puddle she loved and was making the most of it, rolling from side to side with all
four paws waving in the air.

"Trust her," said Emily, "and it's too late to stop her."

She rolled herself the right way up at last, gave
herself a shake, and bounced away into the woods
spraying muddy water from her back as she ran.

"'A featherbrain, but she's fun,'" mimicked Emily.
"We'll have to offer to wash her again when we get
back. I hope Maude and Val won't mind too much.
They must be used to it by now."

"I'm not worried about them," said Neil. "I'm thinking of Mr. and Mrs. Crosby. We have to go right past their house again on the way back."

Emily was quiet for a while. "Isn't there a shortcut we could take? Or a detour?" she said at last.

Neil shook his head. "We could go the long way and come in from the other end of the street, but they'd probably still see us, and so would a lot of other people. We'll just have to hope they're not home." He raised his voice. "Spangle!"

Spangle turned in midair and bounded back to him. Her paws were already on his chest before she remembered what "Sit!" meant. She sat, still panting, her tail wagging, bright, happy eyes turned to his face. In her run through the woods she had romped through leaves, burrs, bushes, and tree roots, and had carried away bits of twig and foliage on the way.

"I don't know what you're laughing at, Spangle," said Neil. "We'll get them all back, Em, before she finds anything else to roll in."

They called for Yap, who was a lot less silky and well-groomed than before, and Ludo, who brought a stick in her mouth and laid it at Emily's feet.

"She's never done that before!" said Neil with admiration. "It looks like she's remembered how to play!" There were a few games of fetch before Emily pointed out that Mrs. Lumley would be wondering where they'd gone to. They did their best to remove the bits of twig and dried leaf from Spangle and Yap.

"It's worse for Yap," said Emily. "He's so hairy and close to the ground, he picks up everything. Ludo's the only sensible one, aren't you, Ludo?"

With all the dogs safely on their leashes, Emily and Neil set off back to Mrs. Lumley's house. Emily pointed out that at least the top of Spangle's head and the tip of her tail were clean, so if Mr. Crosby only saw her passing the garden wall, she might almost look reasonably tidy.

"He'll blow a fuse if he sees the rest of her," said Neil. "She looks even worse out here." The thick mud and straggly dampness, which had seemed messy but natural in the woods, looked appalling in the street. As they turned the corner into Windsor Drive, they glanced nervously at Mr. Crosby's house.

"I can't see anyone," said Neil. "He may not be in."

"He's probably at an upstairs window, with a pair of binoculars trained on number twenty-four," giggled Emily.

"Or putting up lace curtains in the greenhouse," laughed Neil. "And gold taps on the birdbath."

"Come on, let's just sneak past and hope for the best."

It wasn't really that difficult. As Neil had hoped, there was nobody to be seen, so it looked safe to get past unnoticed. Then, from Spangle's throat came a low, warning growl.

Stalking delicately across Mr. Crosby's path, then stopping to rub its face against a trellis, was a calico cat. Neil shortened Spangle's leash.

"Leave it, Spangle. Come!" he commanded in a hushed, urgent voice. He tugged sharply to get her away but bumped into Emily and momentarily softened his grip on the leash.

It was the slack Spangle had been waiting for. With a terrific bound, she yanked the leash from Neil's hands and galloped furiously toward the cat as it dashed for safety under a wooden gate. Spangle leaped over it. Both dog and cat vanished down the side of the house.

Neil and Emily ran after them, down the little side path and into Mr. Crosby's back garden.

"Spangle!" called Neil, looking wildly about. He tried not to raise his voice too much but had to catch Spangle's attention.

"There she is!" said Emily.

Spangle was growling softly, but she had lost interest in the cat. She stood on her hind legs, with her muddy paws against a French window, ignoring Neil and Emily completely. It was Neil's worst nightmare.

"Spangle!" called Neil again, urgently, but not daring to raise his voice. "Spangle, come here now, or we'll all be in trouble!"

The dog's attention was fixed on something on the other side of the glass. Her nose twitched. She began to bark louder and louder. The barks were short and

fierce as Neil and Emily ran to drag her away. Neil looked fearfully in at the window. Then he saw what Spangle was barking at. "Good girl!" he said.

Mr. Crosby, bleary-eyed and puzzled, was wearily pulling himself up from his chair by the fire. He was waking up very slowly and still looked dazed with sleep, and he had not yet noticed what Spangle had smelled and seen.

In the fireplace a guardless coal fire blazed brightly. A glowing coal had tumbled onto the hearthrug, and the rug was already smoldering.

Mr. Crosby was still only half-awake. Neil and

Emily banged on the window and shouted, but the glass muffled the sound.

"Can we get in?" asked Neil urgently, looking for some way to open the French window.

"No!" said Emily. "That's the worst thing to do. A sudden draft could make the whole hearthrug burst into flame. He has to smother the fire." She tried shouting, and Neil joined in. "Mr. Crosby! Wake up!"

CHAPTER TEN

Neil and Emily thought Mr. Crosby would never wake up completely.

Then, at last, he sat up, rubbed his eyes, blinked, and glared at them.

"The hearthrug!" yelled Neil and Emily. They had no time to look apologetic.

Mr. Crosby still looked annoyed and confused as they yelled and tried to point out what was happening. Then the old man saw the danger. He snapped into action and with a swift kick he folded the hearthrug, then stamped on it and went on stamping until every trace of smoldering had been beaten out. He struggled to open the French window, then dragged the rug, ruined and smelling bitterly of smoke, into the yard.

Neil knelt down and put his arms around Spangle. "Well done, you," he said. "Not as silly as they think, are you? Well done, you big, brave dog."

Spangle's mud had been shaken off by now. Much of it had transferred to Neil, and grimy pawprints covered the French window. Neil only hoped that this time nobody would mind. But would Mr. Crosby wonder why they had been in his backyard?

"It was Spangle who noticed what was happening," Neil said hurriedly. "She smelled smoke, and barked, and wouldn't come away from the window."

Mr. Crosby looked at Spangle with something that was almost admiration. Anyone would think he liked dogs. "Well. What a good girl!" he said. "You're brighter than you look!"

"I'm afraid she's not very clean," said Emily anxiously, as Mr. Crosby tentatively put out a hand to pat the bedraggled dog. Compared to Mr. Crosby's spotless sweater, she looked filthy.

"Oh, it's just a bit of fresh mud. I'm not worried about that," he said.

Neil and Emily looked at each other, speechless with astonishment.

"But don't let her into the house," Mr. Crosby added. There was no chance of that. Neil was clinging to her collar with both hands.

"Where did that cat go?" said Emily, looking around and hoping it wouldn't reappear. Now that Spangle was the heroine of the hour, they didn't want her taking off again, especially if it turned out to be Mr. Crosby's cat.

"Cat? What cat?" he demanded. "Was there a cat here? A calico one?"

Neil and Emily nodded and exchanged worried glances.

"It belongs to someone around here, but I've no idea who," Mr. Crosby said. "It's a thorough nuisance. Kills the birds, digs holes in the garden, leaves its visiting card on the lawn. So you've seen it off, have you, Spangle? Well done!" He patted the cleanest part of her head but still got bits of leaf stuck to his sleeve.

"It's not the cat's fault," protested Emily, but Mr. Crosby wasn't listening. Spangle, enjoying the attention, was behaving extremely well, sitting still, and wagging her tail. To Neil's relief she hadn't tried to put her paws on Mr. Crosby's pants yet. He wasn't sure how long this would last, though. Mr. Crosby was looking at the state of his sweater. He might start to regret fussing affectionately with Spangle.

"We'd better get her back to Mrs. Lumley's," Neil said, edging away. "She'll be wondering where we've got to."

"I'll come with you," said Mr. Crosby suddenly. He glanced over his shoulder at his period living room with its elegant fireplace. The bitter tang of smoke lingered in the air. "Could have been a lot worse," he said. "I haven't thanked you two yet, have I?"

As he spoke, Mrs. Crosby came into the room. She looked smaller than ever, and her hands twisted nervously. "George? What's happening? I can smell smoke, and there was a noise — where's the rug? Why are these people here? Oh! Those big dogs!"

"It's all right, dear," said Mr. Crosby. "I've been stupid. I left the guard away from the fireplace and fell asleep in the armchair. If the dog hadn't woken me up, I dread to think what might have happened. You should have seen her, pawing at the window!"

Mrs. Crosby looked at the window with dismay.

"We'll clean it," said Emily quickly.

"Never mind the window," said Mr. Crosby. "We're going to Maude Lumley's. It's time we sorted things out. We're going to talk reasonably, all of us. Val Jennings may be a battle-ax, but I think she's a sensible battle-ax."

He strode briskly ahead of Neil, Emily, and the dogs, and Mrs. Crosby followed them.

Neil and Emily stole a glance at each other. "You don't suppose he's got a twin brother, do you?" said Neil. "He's being really nice."

"If someone had just saved you from your house burning down around you, you'd be really nice to them," said Emily. "I hope it lasts. We can do without a storm at Mrs. Lumley's house. Remember, he's been talking to the police."

"There's Dad!" shouted Neil, as he saw Bob walking down Mrs. Lumley's path. Everything always seemed to be under control when Bob was there.

"Hi," Bob said, and bent down to greet three very enthusiastic dogs. "Hello, Spangle, I see you're still your usual self, spotless and perfectly groomed."

"What are you doing here, Dad?" asked Emily.

"Mrs. Lumley called me up, very worried and confused, with some story about the police calling on Mr. Crosby," Bob replied.

Mr. Crosby coughed and turned his head away guiltily.

"She seemed to think she was about to be prosecuted," Bob went on, "and wanted to know if I'd put in a good word for her if she had to go to court. She seemed so upset. I thought I'd better come by. So, what's going on?"

They told him as quickly as they could. If Mrs. Lumley and the Crosbys were to face each other again, it would be good to have Bob there.

Mrs. Jennings appeared at the front door. "There you are, children. Oh, and Bob! And Mr. and Mrs. Crosby. How *nice* to see you. Maude! Put another three cups on the tray. And fill the teapot."

"That's an excellent idea," said Bob. "And we could do with a towel for Spangle, too. Neil, get out some water for the dogs, would you?"

When they were all seated and drinking tea in the living room, the story of Spangle's rescue was told with great dramatic license by Neil and Emily. Neil had realized that this was an opportunity for the three dogs to keep their home in Windsor Drive.

Yap had settled down on Mrs. Lumley's knee, and Ludo lay stretched out on the floor with her head in Emily's lap. Spangle wriggled about, trying to make herself comfortable beside Neil.

After Neil and Emily had finished, Mr. Crosby cleared his throat and came to the point. "Perhaps I haven't handled things terribly well," he said. "I know you've been upset, Maude, and perhaps with the television and the petition and all that, I may have been a bit heavy-handed."

Mrs. Lumley nodded.

"But I really was worried about what was going on here," continued her neighbor. "There seemed to be more and more dogs every week! You have to admit, sometimes there was a very nasty smell from the yard. We were afraid of it becoming a health hazard, attracting flies. It was shocking! And my wife — you haven't been well, have you, Muriel?"

"Haven't you?" asked Mrs. Lumley. "Oh, I'm sorry, I didn't know that."

"I'm a lot better now," said Mrs. Crosby, and Neil saw that her eyes strayed toward Ludo. "I just had that nasty flu that was going around before Christmas, and it's taken me a while to get over it."

"That isn't all, though, Muriel," said Mr. Crosby. "There's the osteoporosis, too."

"What's that?" asked Emily.

"Brittle bones," her father whispered.

"You'll have to take good care of yourself," said Val Jennings.

"Oh, I just call it wear and tear," said Mrs. Crosby with a shy little laugh.

"It's serious," said Mr. Crosby. "It means her bones could break very easily."

"So that's why you worry about dogs jumping at you in the street!" said Neil. He could understand her fear now.

"I'm so sorry," said Mrs. Lumley. "Of course, we couldn't have that."

"But I like dogs," said Muriel Crosby. "When I was a girl we had a Labrador, a lot like yours. Now I take a good look at her, I can see she's a beauty. Ours was a great one for retrieving."

"Ludo's learning to retrieve things, too," said Neil. He picked up a ball that Yap had been playing with earlier. Ludo watched it with interest. Neil rolled it across the floor, and she padded after it and brought it back to him.

"Try it," said Neil and handed the ball to Mrs. Crosby. "She's very gentle."

"Were the dogs ever out without being under control?" asked Bob.

"They weren't supposed to be," said Mrs. Lumley carefully. "But some of them were very big and strong — big enough to jump the garden wall if anyone ever left a door open. And Yap's so small, small enough to squeeze under the gate if I'm not looking."

"Well, he won't do it while I'm around," said Mrs. Jennings firmly. "I'm so sorry you've had all this worry, Mr. Crosby."

"It has been a worry," said Mr. Crosby. "When the dogs were taken away and the house was cleaned up, I thought everything would be all right. Then these three dogs came back, and I thought we were back where we started."

Neil was watching Mrs. Crosby playing with Ludo. Ludo seemed to have found a friend who would roll the ball for her all afternoon. Mrs. Crosby had been won over, but what about Val Jennings?

"Ludo likes you, Mrs. Crosby," Neil said. "Have you seen that, Mrs. Jennings? There's no harm in the dogs."

Val Jennings looked annoyed. Neil immediately thought that he'd said the wrong thing.

"Why does everybody think I hate dogs?" demanded Mrs. Jennings. "I love dogs! The only reason Harry — he was my husband — and I didn't have a dog was because we were both out at work all day. It would have been cruel to keep one, and I can't bear animal cruelty." She turned to her sister. "That was why I was so upset, Maude. I came here and heard all the stories about the SPCA taking neglected dogs from your house."

Neil blushed. That was exactly how he had felt, too.

"I like dogs, even that hyperactive spaniel," Mrs. Jennings went on. She reached over and patted Spangle's head.

"Val and I have been talking a lot about the dogs," said Mrs. Lumley. "And the future."

"Yes," said Mrs. Jennings. "I sometimes get lonely in my apartment in Eastbourne. I'm going to sell it and come home. Between us, Maude and I should be able to keep this gang under control. And when my apartment is sold, we can afford to do something about the paintwork and the garden. I like gardening."

"I'll be very willing to help with that," said Mr. Crosby eagerly.

"But you shouldn't think we're going in for carriage lamps and stately home fountains," she warned him.

"Sounds fair enough to me," said Bob.

"Does this mean that the police won't press charges?" asked Neil.

"Charges?" asked Mr. Crosby. "I'm sorry, I don't know what you're talking about."

"Sergeant Moorhead," said Neil. "He came to see you today."

"Oh, that!" Mr. Crosby gave an embarrassed little laugh and looked down at his hands. "That's not exactly why he came. I've been down to the police station a lot lately — when your dogs came back, I was furious that the police wouldn't do anything to prevent it, so I decided to make a nuisance of myself until they took action. So he did. He came to have a word with me about . . . um . . ."

"Wasting police time," said Mrs. Crosby. "He said we should stop wasting police time with all the complaints."

Neil bent his head over Spangle to hide the smile creeping across his face. He didn't dare look at Emily in case they both laughed.

A car door banged outside, and Mrs. Jennings looked out a window.

"More company," she said. "Oh, it's that nice SPCA girl. I forgot, she said she'd come today and see how the dogs are doing. I'll get another cup."

Mrs. Lumley answered the door, and Terri came in to the usual noisy chorus of barking.

"Quiet!" ordered Mrs. Jennings with a sharp clap of her hands.

There was silence.

Mrs. Jennings pointed to the floor. Without a sound, all three dogs lay down.

Neil stared, astonished.

"I should think so," Mrs. Jennings said. "Good dogs."

"Well done, Val!" said Bob. "You've done this before, haven't you?"

"I was a teacher for forty years," she replied. "I'm used to giving orders. *And* being obeyed," she said, smiling a little.

"Well, I don't think we're needed here anymore," said Bob, standing up and looking at Neil and Emily. "I'll take you two home. Neil, have you taken your photos?"

"Sorry, I forgot," said Neil. "Can I take the dogs outside, please, for a picture? It's for a school project."

Neil set the dogs on the doorstep while he took his pictures for the school magazine. They all lined up with Ludo in the middle and Yap and Spangle either side.

"Say cheese! You're safe," he whispered to them quietly as he pressed the button on the camera. And, he thought, they did look as if they were smiling!

A week later, Neil ran into the kitchen after school to the usual happy greeting from Sam and Jake. He looked up to see Terri talking to his mom.

"Hi, Neil," she said. "I just came to tell Carole, we're well on the way to finding new homes for all of Mrs. Lumley's dogs."

"Fantastic!" Neil replied.

"Did you ever get your magazine article finished?" she asked.

"I was going to tell you — yes, I did! Even the principal liked it! And it's going to be printed in the magazine!"

"Well done!" Terri bent over and patted Sam. "Do you miss the Lumley dogs at all?"

Neil stroked Jake's soft ears and laughed as the puppy licked him. "Just a bit," he said. "But it's like that with all the dogs who come here. And it was getting difficult, helping with Mrs. Lumley's dogs, and doing homework, and having these two to look after." He looked at his other dog. "I've got more time now with Sam, and that's important. And Jake. Mrs. Lumley's got her best friends, and I've got mine."

He straightened up and picked up a well-chewed Frisbee. "Come on, Jake! Race you around the yard!"